THE TREASURE HUNTERS

Gilda Baxter decides to call unannounced at her fiancé's cottage on a surprise visit . . . only to learn on her arrival that his boat, badly damaged, had been found floating overturned in the bay, and that he is missing — presumed drowned . . . Diana Russell is on a mission to help her twin sister stop a man from blackmailing and ruining her life. For her plan to succeed, she must put herself in great danger — but sometimes best laid plans have a habit of going awry . . .

NORMAN FIRTH

THE TREASURE HUNTERS

Complete and Unabridged

LINFORD
Leicester

First published in Great Britain

First Linford Edition
published 2019

A catalogue record for this book is available
from the British Library.

ISBN 978–1–4448–4143–5

Published by
F. A. Thorpe (Publishing)
Anstey, Leicestershire

Set by Words & Graphics Ltd.
Anstey, Leicestershire
Printed and bound in Great Britain by
T. J. International Ltd., Padstow, Cornwall

This book is printed on acid-free paper

THE TREASURE HUNTERS

1

The Wolf in the Train

Through half-closed eyelashes, she watched him, wondering why he hadn't taken his eyes off her from the moment he entered the train.

She had to admit he was strikingly handsome. Not a hair was out of place and his eyes were so dark that it was impossible to distinguish their colour. But the thin line of his moustache did nothing to disguise his mouth — it intensified it rather than otherwise. His mouth was cruel and wicked.

Yet it was his eyes that really hypnotised Gilda Baxter. They held an insolent assurance which seemed to indicate that their owner only had to beckon with his little finger to get whatever he wanted — at least as far as women were concerned. When she had first met his bold stare, a hot flush had crept under her make-up.

His gaze was full of meaning — and she was alone in the carriage with him!

He continued to stare, and, every second, his eyes had become more confident of victory.

She forced herself to look out of the window and tried to forget the presence of the man opposite by thinking of Martin. How surprised Martin would be when he opened the door of the cottage to find her standing on the step.

Gilda tried to analyse her reasons for paying her fiancé this unexpected visit. Surely it was only because she was in love with Martin that she was going to Knapp Cove. But no — she was going because she was possessed by an overwhelming curiosity.

It was exactly a week since Martin had driven to London for the day. He had called at her office, had taken her out to lunch, and never had she known him so excited. He had talked extravagantly of the future.

'We're going to be married within a few weeks,' he had announced. 'After that we shall have everything we want. You'll see!'

'But you can't have sold your novel already,' she had protested. 'You can't have half-finished it yet.' It was because of the novel he intended to write that Martin Kane had buried himself in the lonely cottage on Knapp Cove. She asked: 'What's all the secret about?'

He had given her an even greater shock then. Out of his pocket he had taken a small stone that glittered and flashed in the light from the restaurant windows. A large diamond!

'What do you think of this?' he had demanded.

Her mouth had opened in wonder.

'Is it a diamond?' she had asked. 'If so, it must be worth thousands and thousands of pounds.'

'Worth thousands anyway,' he had said complacently. 'It's one of the reasons I've come to town. I've got to buy or hire a diving suit and . . . But the rest really is a secret. I can't tell you.' He glanced at his watch. 'When I'm with you, time simply races away. If I don't hurry I'll lose my chance of getting a diving suit. I'm late for my appointment as it is.'

There had been little time to question him further. Gilda had tried but he had put her off. Then she had demanded to know what the mystery was about.

'All in good time, darling,' he had said. 'But you can hand in your notice at the office any time now. Within a few weeks we're going to be on our honeymoon — a more wonderful honeymoon than we've ever imagined.'

All through that week she had wondered about that diamond. How had Martin come by it? And why had he been so secretive? Then, only yesterday, Mr. Ledburn, her employer, had sent for her.

'I have to go to the Continent,' he had said, 'and I shall be away for about a fortnight. There's nothing you can do while I'm away, so you may as well have the time off. Take a holiday and enjoy yourself.'

It was then she decided to go to Knapp Cove. Where else would she go when she had a fortnight's freedom? Naturally she wanted to be near Martin; also she wanted to probe the mystery behind the diamond.

She came out of her reverie as she

noticed that the train was running along the coast. The presence of the man with the gimlet eyes still persisted. All the time, she knew that the man opposite was staring at her.

There was, of course, some excuse for him. Most men stared at Gilda. He was looking at a girl clad in a summer frock that did full justice to the lines of a perfect figure. Her fair hair was a halo round her head and her eyes were the bluest he had ever seen. People said that Gilda Baxter was as lovely as a film star. But there was much more than mere loveliness in Gilda's face — the tilt of a determined little chin gave it character.

The man in the train ought to have taken warning from the tilt of that determined little chin — perhaps he did.

The train stopped at Knapp Junction. Gilda hoped that someone else would get in the carriage so that she wouldn't be alone with this glaring Romeo. No one came to her carriage, however, and the train chugged off again.

Despite herself, she looked across at him. Yes — he was still staring. It seemed to her now that there was the sudden suggestion of excitement in his eyes. Knapp station was the terminus — the train would go no further. Was that expression of excitement due to the fact that he now knew she was bound for Knapp? Was he now playing for time? Did he intend to follow up his interest later when they got off the train?

He took a gold cigarette case from his pocket and snapped it open.

'May I offer you a cigarette?' he enquired.

His voice was soft, like a caress. Gilda tried to look forbidding, but only succeeded in looking more glamorous.

'No, thank you,' she answered. 'I shall be getting out in a moment.'

He closed the case without taking a cigarette himself.

'I didn't expect you to smoke,' he said with casual familiarity. 'But all this time I have been wondering if your voice was in keeping with the rest of you. It seemed impossible that it could be. Yet it is — perfectly in keeping.'

His almost stilted words had been

intended as a compliment. They were meant to please her. Yet Gilda felt that she had been insulted. She tried to think of a snappy come-back which would crush him. But he went on speaking:

'There are very few visitors at Knapp Cove these days. Are you on holiday?'

'For a few days,' she forced herself to answer. After all, it might be wiser to be polite. He looked strong and ruthless — the kind of man who would take kisses by force.

His eyebrows went up a little at her slight hesitation, but he made no comment.

'A car will be meeting me,' he said, 'I shall be charmed to give you a lift.'

Quickly Gilda shook her head.

'Someone will be meeting me at the station, too,' she said, and, at that moment, the train jerked to a stop.

He held the door open for her and then handed out her suitcase.

'I'm so sorry I can't be of further help,' he said. 'However, I have the consolation of knowing that Knapp Cove is a small place. We are bound to meet again. So, at the moment, I will just wish you 'good-day'.'

Of course there was no one to meet her. But, having pretended there was, she waited on the station. She watched the stranger pass through the ticket barrier and saw him climb into a large saloon car. Even then she waited until the car was out of sight before approaching the barrier.

'May I leave my case with you?' she asked the ticket collector. 'I will call back for it sometime tonight.'

'Anything to oblige you, miss.'

She had a long walk ahead of her — three miles at least along the rough, boulder-studded path over the cliffs. The thought of meeting her handsome fiancé made her eyes sparkle. How surprised he would be to see her and how delighted! They would spend a wonderful fortnight together exchanging a million kisses. He would be sure to tell her now all about the diamond and why it had suddenly become possible for them to get married so quickly. Only a few weeks ago, they had decided it would take another year at least for them to save enough money to set up a home. Well, soon her feminine, overwhelming curiosity would be satisfied. She would know his mysterious secret.

Gilda left the tiny hamlet of Knapp behind her and started along the cliff walk. She recalled her first visit to the cottage. She had been able to stay only a few days then but they had had a wonderful time. This time it was going to be even more wonderful because soon she was going to be married to Martin, and then she would be his utterly.

She walked the first two miles and then came out to the cove. Surely this was the quietest, loneliest place in the whole of the country. Down near the water's edge she saw a tiny cottage. That was the fisherman's cottage. What was his name? Elias Cobb — that was it! She had met the dour fisherman once with Martin, but Elias had very little to say. That wasn't to be wondered at — living in such a lonely place he would have little opportunity for conversation.

She saw the cottage-cum-log-cabin at

the other side of the cove — saw the thin line of smoke from the chimney, and her heart leapt. That was Martin's cottage, and, judging by the smoke, he was at home. She ran down the slope into the cove. Across the shingle she went, and now she was climbing the well-remembered path. Would he see her — would he come running to meet her with his arms wide open?

But, to her disappointment, the door remained closed. Reaching it, she lifted the knocker and let it fall. The sound went echoing through the cottage. She waited but nothing happened. Perhaps, after all, he was out somewhere in the cove.

She knocked again, and this time heard footsteps. The door opened.

'Darling!' she began, and then the words were checked on her lips.

It wasn't Martin who had opened the door. It was the human wolf who had been in the train!

His surprise seemed almost as great as her own.

'Where's Martin Kane?' she asked. 'Is — he at home? I — I'm his fiancé.'

For the moment the man went on staring. Then his teeth showed in a flashing smile.

'And to think that we travelled down together!' he said. 'What an idiot I was not to make further enquiries about you. I came, of course, by the Tedworth Road. But, really — my manners are atrocious. I'm actually keeping you standing on the doorstep. Do come in.'

'Where's Martin?' she asked briskly.

'He's out in the cove somewhere,' the man answered casually. 'I'm expecting him back any moment.'

She crossed the threshold, less anxious now.

'I was so sure we would meet again,' he said with a smile. 'But I never imagined it would be so soon. Let me introduce myself. My name's Hugo Meyer.'

'I am Gilda Baxter,' she said formally.

'So it's Gilda,' he said. 'I'd been wondering. Even the name suits you to perfection.' He moved nearer. 'I don't suppose for a moment that Martin has told you about me? I've come down here to help him in his work.'

She felt her heart sink. If this man was going to stay at the cottage, then she knew she would loathe the fortnight — not enjoy it. Again he was looking at her in that bold, speculating way that made her shiver. She wondered how Martin ever came to have anything to do with such a slinky specimen as this.

She talked — just for the sake of talking. Anything to make him turn his eyes away from her.

'But I thought Martin was only working on his novel,' she said. 'He hasn't told me about any other work though he hinted at something mysterious — '

She couldn't be sure, but, for the moment, his eyes seemed to fill with suspicion. Then he shrugged his shoulders.

'There is other work,' he said slowly. 'Very exciting work, too. But I'll let Martin tell you about that when he comes in. And, while you're waiting, I'll make you a cup of tea. I'm sure you'll like that.'

He turned away. As he did so, there was a loud knock at the front door.

'This seems to be our day for visitors,'

he said. 'Excuse me.'

He went into the passage, and she heard him open the door. A harsh voice came to her — a voice she remembered. It belonged to Elias Cobb, the fisherman.

'Is Mr. Martin Kane at home?' the voice enquired.

'No,' was the reply. 'I understand he went out fishing in his boat this afternoon.'

Gilda's heart stood still, and the room seemed to revolve around her.

'Then — God rest his soul — he's drowned!' came the voice of Elias Cobb. 'I've just collected his overturned boat which was going out with the tide.'

2

Scream of Terror

The words echoed in Gilda's mind.

'I've been afraid of it right from the very beginning,' the fisherman was saying. 'Mr. Kane was always too venturesome. Time and time again I've warned him about the current. Once a boat goes into it, it can never get out again. And there's a big swell on today, too. One side of his boat is stove right in, so it must have smashed into the cliffs before turning over.'

Gilda began running out of the sitting-room and into the passage. She pushed Hugo Meyer to one side and faced Elias Cobb.

'It can't be true,' she said frantically. 'Martin couldn't drown; he's much too strong a swimmer. He wouldn't drown just because a boat turned over. He'd swim to shore, I tell you.'

Cobb's mouth dropped as he stared at her in astonishment. Awkwardly he made to doff his cap.

'This is Miss Baxter,' Meyer said quietly. 'Mr. Kane's fiancée.'

'Martin isn't dead,' echoed Gilda. 'I know he isn't dead.'

Of course he wasn't dead. He was the strongest swimmer she had ever known. Why, only on her last visit to the cove, he had come to her aid. That had been after a very long swim, and he had been almost as fresh then as when he had started. Again she experienced that wonderful feeling of relief when his strong arm had gone round her. She felt quite convinced that the fisherman — not knowing Martin's swimming powers — had jumped to a tragic conclusion.

'I'm sorry, miss,' said the fisherman, 'but I'm afraid it ain't good news. As soon as I'd righted his boat and made it fast, I shouted for him. I rowed all 'round the cove, too. But there was no sign of him — no sign at all. If he was swimming there'd be some sign of him for sure.' The dour fisherman rubbed his head. 'I reckon he must have got knocked out and then drowned.'

Meyer's arm went round her shoulders, and she didn't even notice it.

'I'll go down and see for myself,' Meyer said. 'You had better lie down Gilda, and . . . '

'No!' she said firmly. 'I — I must come with you. I couldn't stay here. And I — I still don't believe that — that anything has happened to Martin.'

Elias Cobb shook his head gravely.

'I pulled the boat up on the shingle,' he said. 'You'd better come and look at it.'

He led the way down the narrow path. And there — lying on the shingle — was Martin's boat. As Cobb had said, one side was stove in.

'It's a miracle she didn't sink,' commented Hugo Meyer. 'The boat must have hit the cliffs with terrific force.'

Gilda looked across the tiny bay. The sea appeared to be calm enough but there was a line of foam where it lapped the cliffs.

Elias Cobb noted the direction of her gaze.

'The current is just beyond that streak of white rock, miss,' he said. 'It's about there that the boat must have hit the cliffs. And — and even if Mr. Kane was a strong swimmer it wouldn't help him much. The strongest swimmer would be pulled down by the undertow today.'

Yet Martin had once swum along the base of the cliffs, and so had she. That had been the afternoon when they had swum out to the cave. It was on the return journey that her strength had suddenly given out and Martin had come to her aid. Martin had often swum out to the cave and he had never mentioned anything about the undertow.

Suddenly her eyes were wide. The cave! But, of course.

'There's a cave just beyond that streak of white rock,' she exclaimed. 'If the boat did crash into the rock, the cave's the first place Martin would make for. I've been inside it myself — it's easy to reach it at high tide.'

Both men stared at her.

'You think he might be inside the cave?' said Meyer slowly. 'I doubt it.'

'We must make sure,' Gilda said. 'If Mr. Cobb will row me across . . . '

'We'll all go,' said Hugo Meyer.

Elias Cobb drew back.

'I don't like venturing too near the cliffs today,' he growled. 'I know this bit of coast and . . . '

'We must make sure,' snapped Meyer. 'Hurry.'

The fisherman shrugged his shoulders and then crossed to his own boat. Slowly — incredibly slowly it seemed to Gilda — Elias Cobb rowed across the bay. As she strained her eyes Gilda felt her last hope dwindle away. If Martin had reached the cave surely he would have been standing in the entrance now, waving to them. She could see the dark opening quite clearly; nobody was standing inside it. But perhaps Martin was injured — perhaps he was lying inside the cave, out of sight.

They were near the cliffs now. Despite the line of white foam, it didn't seem to her that the waves were striking the rocks with any particular force.

'We're out of the current here, miss,' Elias Cobb told her. 'I wouldn't have risked coming to the cave otherwise.'

Still nobody appeared in the cave entrance.

'Martin! Martin!'

But only the wheeling gulls answered her call.

Gilda half rose to her feet. She must see for herself — she must make sure. But Hugo Meyer pulled her back and held her fast.

'Not you, my dear,' he said, and the caress in his voice sickened her. 'These rocks are far too slippery and we don't want an accident to happen to you. This is a job for Cobb.'

The fisherman looked doubtfully at the cave entrance.

'Make sure you hold the boat fast,' he snapped. 'I don't want it to be swept into the current. You'd better hang on to this rock, sir.'

Hugo Meyer held on with one hand; the other held Gilda in her seat.

'I can manage,' he said. 'Just leave her to me.'

The tide was on the turn, and the level of the water had fallen below the entrance to the cave. Elias Cobb climbed over the slippery surface with some difficulty, and Gilda watched him disappear into the darkness beyond the opening. Time went by; no sound came to her, and slowly she began to lose hope.

The fisherman reappeared and he scrambled back to the boat. He shook his head.

'I've covered every yard of the cave,' he said. 'There's nobody there.'

A low cry escaped Gilda and she hid her face in her hands. Then — then it was true. Martin was dead — even now the tide was sweeping his body out to sea. She had arrived just an hour too late. If only she had caught an earlier train, this — this would not have happened.

Meyer looked at her tensely.

'Better row for your cottage,' said Hugo Meyer to Cobb. 'Your sister is the person to take care of Miss Baxter now.'

'Eh?' queried the fisherman. 'Oh — yes.'

He started to row across the bay. Afterwards Gilda never remembered that return journey. One moment she was outside the cave, heart-broken, and the next moment, she was dazedly being led by Meyer up the flagged path to Elias Cobb's cottage.

The door opened and a girl stood there. In that quiet cove she seemed entirely out of place; her dark beauty was of Southern Seas. Despite her grief Gilda realised this. There was nothing about the strange girl's dress to denote a fisherman's sister. The dark crimson gown she wore bore the stamp of fashion.

It seemed to Gilda, too, that Elias Cobb's sister gazed at her with a strange hostility.

'You'd better tell her what has happened,' Hugo Meyer said.

Elias Cobb hurried forward, and explained . . .

The other girl welcomed her.

'You poor dear,' she said. 'What a terrible, terrible thing! But come in and sit down. The kettle is on the hob and I can soon make tea. You'll come in too, Mr. Meyer?'

He shook his head.

'Later,' he answered. 'I've got to see the

police.' Meyer edged away from the door. 'I'll leave Miss Baxter in your care.'

Elias and his sister took her into the kitchen and they showed her rough kindness. She swallowed some tea but that was all. After that she wanted to go back to the cove — to start another search. Gently they talked her out of it.

'You must lie down,' said Elias's sister. 'Luckily we can put you up for the night. Shall I bring your things down from the cottage?'

Gilda told her that her suitcase was still at the railway station.

'Elias shall get it for you,' she said.

Gilda wondered about Elias Cobb's sister. She did not speak like the other fisher folk. Hers was an educated voice and somewhere in it was the hint of a foreign accent. Maybe it was only because she had travelled.

When Elias Cobb returned with her suitcase, Gilda went to bed. But there was no sleep for her — only the numb ache of emptiness. For hours it seemed she lay staring unseeingly at the ceiling. Then there was a knock at the door and Hugo

Meyer came in. In his hands was a large bunch of flowers.

'I've brought you these,' he said, in his caressing voice. 'I thought they would brighten up the room a little.'

Her fingers clutched the coverlet.

'Is there — is there any more news?'

'No news,' he answered. 'I've given the alarm, and a police launch is out in the bay now. But it would be foolish to hope. I can't tell you how much I feel for you. It's been a shocking blow.'

Before she could realise his intention he had taken one of her hands and was squeezing her fingers. He intended it as a comforting gesture. But the mere touch of his hand made her head reel.

After he had gone, she lay more wide-eyed than ever. For the first time since Elias Cobb's arrival at the cottage she found herself able to think clearly. She remembered Martin's visit to London. Why had he been so excited then? What was the mystery of the diamond? And who exactly was Hugo Meyer?

The thought of him made her shudder; her instinctive dislike on first seeing him had become something a thousand times stronger, despite his apparent kindness. Why hadn't Martin told her about him? She had thought that she fully enjoyed Martin's confidence, yet never once had he mentioned Hugo Meyer although the latter talked of Martin as though he was the oldest of old friends.

Another thing: Hugo Meyer had known nothing of her. He had shown obvious surprise when she had introduced herself as Martin's fiancée. If Meyer had known Martin at all well, then he must surely have heard of her. It was strange — very strange. Her hands tightened grimly. No matter what happened now she would remain at the cove until she had solved the mystery.

She listened for a long time. There was no sound. Both Cobb and his sister must be asleep now. It ought to be easy to leave the cottage without disturbing them. Quietly she dressed herself and then she opened her case to take out the light coat she had brought with her. Wrapping it round her she opened her door and stole quietly down the staircase.

Everything was made easy for her — the front door had neither been locked nor bolted.

Outside a pale moon was swimming in a watery sky and there was a hint of rain in the air. The sea gleamed, unfriendly and menacing. Nothing moved upon it; the police launch must have given up the search long ago.

Slowly she went on until she came to Martin's boat. Her fingers gripped one of the sides and her knuckles showed white. The boat wasn't very badly damaged after all. The top of one side had been knocked in, but she was sure the boat would still float. Yet, because of it, Martin had gone to his death. Of course, the boat had been floating upside-down when it had been seen by Elias Cobb. It must have over-turned on hitting the rocks. And — and Martin might have been flung against the rocks — he might have been stunned. That would explain his failure to save himself.

She turned and looked towards the cottage. A light was still burning in the sitting-room window. So Hugo Meyer hadn't yet gone to bed! What was he doing at this late hour? The temptation came to her to creep up to the window and to peer inside.

She made to move forward — and then suddenly stopped. Footsteps were coming down the path from the cottage. And — and there was more than one person. She had thought Hugo Meyer was alone in the cottage.

Two vague figures reached the shingle and then they turned at a tangent. They were too far away — too vague and indistinct — for her to recognise them. But Hugo Meyer wasn't one of them — she was sure of that. Her eyes followed them down to the water edge and then she saw two figures push a boat into the water, and the faint creak of oars came to her ears.

Gilda's pulses began to race. Who were the two men in the boat? Why had they been to see Hugo Meyer? They must be part and parcel of the mystery she had set out to solve. It must have been some sixth sense that had prompted her to venture out that night. If only she could discover where they were bound. If she could keep them in sight . . .

Even as the thought was born, a dark cloud swept over the moon. The sea was blotted out as though at a wave of a magician's wand. It started to rain — great heavy drops that stung her face.

This was the cruelest luck. She still tried to pierce the darkness — tried to ignore the rain. But it became a downpour and she was forced to think of shelter. She found it under the ledge of a huge boulder not far away.

For perhaps half-an-hour she crouched there. Then the shower ceased as abruptly as it had begun and the moon swept back into the sky. The surface of the bay was now empty; there was no sign of the boat. Then Gilda's hands flew to her breasts, and, wide-eyed, she stared out to sea.

From somewhere out there across the dark water had come a scream of terror!

3

Drugged Tea

She held her breath as she listened, but the scream did not sound again. What was happening out there? Who had been responsible for that terrible cry?

It had come from the direction of the cliffs, but there was nothing to be seen there. There was nothing but heavy, black shadows, and silence. But someone had screamed — someone who needed help.

All of a sudden Gilda felt herself possessed by a demon of anxiety. She must reach the cliffs. She hardly knew what she thought; she only knew she could not remain on the beach. Running to Martin's boat she seized the stern and tried to pull it to the water. Part of one side might be stove in, but she was sure it would float. She could make it safer by sitting far over on the other side. The boat was heavy and wouldn't give to her tugs immediately.

Hurrying footsteps sounded on the shingle, but she was straining so hard that she heard nothing until a dark shadow fell across her.

She started and looked up — at Hugo Meyer!

'Gilda!' he exclaimed. 'What the dickens do you think you're doing?'

Gilda fought down her fear of him. He was a strong man, and he would be physically capable of helping her with the boat. Out at the cliffs someone was in trouble . . .

'I couldn't sleep,' she heard herself saying. 'That's why I came out. And just now I heard a cry. It was a terrible cry, like someone in pain. It seemed to come from the cliffs.'

Some sixth sense warned her to say nothing of the two men she had seen.

'You poor child!' Meyer said smoothly. 'This has been a terrible day for you. No wonder you couldn't sleep. I can't say I blame you for imagining things.'

'But I tell you there was a scream. It — it sounded like someone in terror and . . . '

He shook his head.

'It was just the cry of a sea-bird,' he stated. 'I made the same mistake the first night I came here. Why, I actually got out of bed. In fact I heard it several times and each time I got up. Then Martin explained. He said it was a large bird that perched on the promontory every night.'

She knew that he was lying! A man had been responsible for that cry — not a bird. But, even if she argued with him, it would make no difference. He came round the boat to her.

'Good gracious!' he exclaimed. 'How wet you are! If you stand about like this you'll catch your death of cold and then I shall feel it's my fault.'

'I don't want to go back.'

He took her arm.

'Nonsense!' he, said. 'I insist that you let me take care of you. You'll come right up to the cottage and I'll make you something hot. You can dry your coat as well.'

Her first impulse was to tear away her arm from his grasp. As always his nearness filled her with loathing. Yet, despite her fear of him, she found that she could still think clearly.

He had lied to her about that terrible cry. Of that she was sure. She was also sure that he did not want her to take Martin's boat out on the bay.

But she was determined to get to the bottom of the mystery. To do that she would have to make use of Hugo Meyer. And, if she wanted to find out all about him, then she must force herself to be friendly and that might lead to all sorts of dangers. Somehow she forced a smile.

'Well, perhaps I would like a cup of tea,' she said. 'I suppose there's no use in waiting here in the rain.'

She was sure relief showed itself in his dark eyes.

'Now you're being sensible!'

Still holding her arm, he piloted her across the shingle and along a narrow path. Then for the second time, she entered Martin's cottage in the company of Hugo Meyer.

'Give me your coat,' he said. 'There's still a fire in the kitchen range and your coat will soon dry. I'll put the kettle on, too.'

He took her coat into the kitchen. Presently he was back, and he seated himself facing her. He talked about trivial things, but she quickly realised his mind was not on what he was saying. His eyes were restless and the least sound caused him to turn his head. Was he afraid that someone might come to the cottage while she was still there?

He got up after a while.

'I can hear the kettle singing. I'll go and make the devil's brew.'

Gilda stood up.

'Let me,' she said. 'I enjoy making tea.'

She could have sworn then that alarm flashed into his eyes. Then he pulled himself together and, chuckling, forced her back to the settee.

'Certainly not,' he said. 'You are my guest. I insist that you stay where it's warm.'

He walked into the kitchen, and the door half closed behind him. Gilda discovered she was trembling. She knew the danger she faced in trying to vamp a man who was obviously a wolf. She looked anxiously towards the half-closed door. Acting on impulse she came to her feet and, quietly, she crossed to the door. Slowly her fingers eased it open.

She saw him standing with his back towards her and he was pouring tea into two cups. He put the teapot down and then a subdued chuckle escaped him. Gilda's eyes grew wider still. She saw him take a tiny white packet from his pocket — saw him tear off the edge. Then, deliberately, he poured the contents into one of the cups and, as he did so, he chuckled again.

Gilda went back to the settee. Never had she needed self-control as she needed it now. Hugo Meyer intended to drug her! That had been his purpose in inviting her to the cottage for a cup of tea. And after she had been drugged — what then?

He came back into the room, smiling.

'Here we are,' he said. 'You'd better drink it while it's hot. It'll do you all the good in the world.'

She took the cup and actually lifted it to her lips.

'It's a little too hot,' she said. 'I'll have to let it cool.'

He continued to smile at her, and gently sipped at his own tea.

The expression in his eyes was more penetrating than ever before. She knew he was gloating over something.

Suddenly she shivered.

'I'm cold,' she murmured.

'Better drink your tea now,' he urged.

'There's a draught from the window,' she said. 'I wonder if you would mind closing it.'

'Of course not.'

The moment his back was turned she reached over and poured the contents of her cup into a flower-pot which stood on a small side-table. When he turned, the cup was still at her lips.

She pretended to drain it.

'*Mmmmm!* That was good,' she remarked and smiled at him.

He took the cup away from her.

'We'll give your coat a little longer to dry,' he said; 'and then I'll take you back to Cobb's cottage.'

Again he talked of trivial things as though he was trying to stop her thinking of Martin's death. But she scarcely heard a word, for she had made up her mind to a plan of action and she was screwing her courage to the sticking point.

Hugo Meyer had tried to drug her. Well, she would let him think that he had succeeded. If she pretended to be unconscious, he might talk freely in front of her; she might also discover the identity of the two men who had been in the cottage with him. Martin's death was bound up with the mystery of the cave — of that she was convinced. If she could avenge Martin, then she would be willing to run any risk.

She became aware of his eyes again — grew conscious he was waiting for something to happen.

She placed a hand on her mouth.

'I feel so tired,' she said. 'So — so very tired.'

Slowly then she started to slip sideways until she lay elegantly along the settee with her eyes closed. She heard him move and realised he was bending over her.

'Some of them pass out more quickly than you did, my dear,' he said. 'And now, I shan't have to worry about you for a very long time.'

She felt one hand go round her shoulders. Gilda marveled at herself. Despite the horror that flooded through her she forced herself to lie limp.

This was the supreme test. Could she bluff him that she was unconscious? At all costs she must let him think that he had succeeded in drugging her. She stifled her nausea as he held her nearer. His hot breath fanned her cheek. Next moment his mouth pressed firmly against hers, and she had to exert herself to prevent her lips going tense in protest.

His hands had now moved round to the back of her neck. Then they stroked her hair — and at last she was free from that voluptuous mouth. But only for a moment. A second later, he was kissing her eyes, her forehead and the little hollow in her chin.

'Lovely one,' he murmured to himself. 'You are my slave. I could give you all the love in the world. A million kisses would be mine for the taking . . . But what's the use? You can't respond to my kisses, but someday you will. Even if I kissed you by force, and you resisted — well, that would be more satisfying than kissing a beautiful, lifeless doll. I'll wait until you come round, my darling, then I'll make you love me — yes, by force, if necessary.'

Gilda experienced a new horror. Was she never going to be free of this man's dreadful attentions? He was mad, of course — mad with thwarted passion. Why, here he was talking to himself, like a lunatic.

Unexpectedly she felt herself being released, and guessed that Hugo Meyer was looking down at her possessively. Again he spoke.

'I'm glad you came to Knapp Cove,' he said. 'Little did I think that, when I came here, I was destined to hold you in my arms. For you, my dear, are the most desirable woman I have ever known . . . Pleasant dreams!'

She heard the door click shut behind him. Oh, the wonderful relief of being able to open her eyes!

Somehow she must force herself to forget the memory of the last few hateful minutes. But there was consolation — so far her plan had succeeded. Hugo Meyer firmly believed she was under the power of the drug. All she could do now was to lie and wait.

The long minutes dragged by. Then the door opened again, and quickly she closed her eyes. She realised Meyer was carrying one of the small lamps.

She knew, too, when his face came close to hers, that he was going to be dangerous.

'I had to make sure,' he murmured. 'No — there's nothing wrong with your breathing; I didn't give you too strong a dose after all.'

She lay motionless as he bent nearer still.

'You're beautiful,' he said, and his voice trembled. 'I've a good mind to wake you up. Why should I wait before I take your kisses?'

There were sudden sounds outside the cottage and then a knocking at the front door. Hugo Meyer swore colourfully and then he hurried from the room.

4

The Woman Who Paid

Voices came to her from the next room. Sitting up, Gilda listened. Who was Meyer's visitor? Perhaps her ordeal was going to pay immediate dividends.

Suddenly she leapt from the settee and crossed on tip-toe to the door. Gently her hand turned the door knob and she opened the door an inch.

'You fool!' said a strange man's voice. 'Why did you have to bring that girl here, Hugo?'

Meyer's amused laugh came to her.

'I had to make sure of her,' he said. 'And, in making sure, there was no reason why I shouldn't enjoy myself.'

There was a fierce exclamation at that.

'Women! Women! It's always women where you're concerned. I tell you I'm getting too scared to work with you. Didn't that blonde teach you a lesson?

You'd never have gone down for five years if she hadn't blown the gaff.'

Meyer laughed again.

'She paid!' he said. 'Looking back now I sometimes think that making her pay was worth five years.'

The strange voice sounded again.

'What about Anna Berg? You can't run any risks where she's concerned. If she suspects that you've designs on this girl, there's no telling . . . '

'To blazes with Anna Berg!' interrupted Hugo Meyer. 'I've known her too long; I grew tired of her ages ago. I'm only waiting to get this job finished and then I'll get rid of her. If she tries to cause trouble, then I'm afraid she will just quietly disappear.'

Gilda's hand went to her throat. What a risk she had taken in pretending to be drugged — in placing herself at Meyer's mercy! But she was glad she had done so — glad! How, otherwise, could she have heard this vital conversation?

'You're going to leave this Baxter girl alone,' insisted the strange voice. 'This is the biggest thing we've ever handled and we've run all the risks we're going to run. You'll get rid of this girl tomorrow — you'll send her back to London. Why, you crazy fool, if we clean up here — as we shall clean up — all the most beautiful women in the world will be at your feet.'

Hugo Meyer laughed again.

'At the moment I'm not interested in the world's most beautiful women,' he said. 'I'm only interested in this girl. As you know, there have been many women in my life. But not one of them has ever appealed to me as this girl does. From the moment I first set eyes on her, I wanted her kisses. In that very first moment I decided that I would win her — that nothing should stop me. And now she is sharing this cottage with me. What could be more pleasant? Now don't you worry that she will be a danger to our plans. I have a way with women as you know. She will be a most willing sweetheart, Max — of that I assure you.'

'The blonde was willing enough,' said Max. 'Very, very willing. But she still sent you down for five years.'

'I'll admit she was a mistake,' said

Meyer. 'But it was a mistake that won't be repeated.'

'Let her go back to London,' pleaded the other man. 'She's dynamite. You've only to look at her to see the girl's got spirit.'

'Exactly! The kind of spirit I like.' Hugo chuckled. 'But then, of course, you wouldn't understand. You've probably never known the strange thrill of holding a beautiful, struggling girl in your arms. Pah! The girls who give their kisses freely are ten-a-penny. It's the lovely girl who resists that I want. Her kisses are worth taking.'

'Women'll be your undoing, Hugo,' the other man said deeply. 'Don't be a fool. Pack her off to town in the morning.'

Hugo Meyer shook his head.

'No, Max,' he said quietly, 'I shan't send her back to London tomorrow. For one thing, it's very necessary that we keep her here. We still don't know if she has been told anything about this business. That is something we must find out — our safety depends upon it. So I shall keep her here.'

The man, Max, was speaking again.

'Of course!' he exclaimed. 'The very thing! Why didn't I think of it before? I'll take her over to the cave tonight — why should we waste time? We'll . . . '

'No!' rapped Meyer and his voice was no longer smooth; it was a snarl. 'Tonight we'll go alone. I've no intention of ill-using her until I have to.'

Then apprehension came back to Gilda. Her soul grew sick as she visualised what might happen if Meyer had his way with her.

The other man still tried to protest, but Meyer cut him short.

'There is one thing also that you forget,' he snapped. 'This man has proved to be obstinate; so far he has told us nothing. If he fails to speak tonight, then we will confront him with the girl. He is in love with her, remember. You may take it from me, Max — and I have had much experience of love — he won't remain obstinate long once he knows the girl is in our hands.'

All in a flash Gilda was living in a new world — a wonderful new world! Right from the beginning she had refused to let herself think that Martin was really dead. From the moment Hugo Meyer had opened the cottage door she had known that something suspicious was going on. She had suspected that he had been lying. How right she had been to come to the cottage — to risk the smooth menace of Hugo Meyer! Now she had learned the one thing in the world she had wanted to know. *Martin was alive!* Somewhere they were holding him prisoner. So her life's happiness was not at an end!

Then apprehension came back to Gilda. She must be more careful than she had ever been in her life before. Not for one single moment must she let them suspect that she knew their secret. But, if Meyer was infatuated with her, then she would turn that infatuation to her own ends. No matter what risks she ran she would force him to tell her about Martin.

'We're wasting time, Hugo,' came Max's voice. 'I'm a fool to try and reason with you where a woman's concerned.'

There was a moment's silence; then the front door slammed.

Gilda ran to the door in time to see them disappearing down the path. There was a faint moon and, for once, she didn't welcome its silvery brightness. If the two men looked back, she was bound to be seen because she dare not let them out of her sight. If she could only succeed in following them, they would lead her to Martin's prison. Perhaps, that very night, she would be able to rescue him.

Down the path she went. The two men came in sight again, and she saw they were crossing the shingle. She saw the boat at the water's edge and her heart stood still. So they were going to row out to sea! If they did that, she would not be able to follow. Was she going to lose the trail leading to Martin almost as soon as she had picked it up?

They did climb into the boat. Clasping her hands, Gilda stood helpless. The boat would disappear around the headland, and after that she would not be able to see it again.

But wait! The boat was not headed for the headland — it was being rowed towards the cliffs. Directly ahead of it she could vaguely distinguish that streak of white rock. The cave! They were rowing towards the cave.

But Martin could not be a prisoner inside the cave. Elias Cobb had entered it that afternoon. It had been empty then. But they could have taken Martin there afterwards: once the cave had been searched, nobody, even if they suspected Martin was still alive, would think of searching there again. And the man, Max, had said that they were late — that they must hurry to Martin. Yes, he was a prisoner inside the cave. She was sure of it now.

She had swam to the cave once before; therefore she could swim to it again. She had to make sure. Already she was pulling off her clothes. Then, clad only in a single garment, she stood at the water's edge for a moment like some sea sprite.

The shingle beach sloped steeply, and two steps took her out of her depth. She swam strongly but, even in her haste, she remembered the course over which Martin had previously led her. In order to avoid the dangerous current she must swim in a kind of semi-circle. It made the distance much longer, but it was the only safe route.

When she had last attempted the swim she had been exhausted on reaching the cliffs. Now, when her fingers clutched the gunwale of Cobb's boat, she had no feeling of tiredness. Her anxiety had conquered fatigue.

The boat was empty and there was no sign of the two men. But, from somewhere far inside the cave, showed the glimmer of a light. She eased herself round the corner. Gilda saw a storm lantern burning inside the cave; it stood high on a ledge so that everything was thrown into sharp relief. Hugo Meyer was there and so was the man, Max. Both were standing with their backs towards her. But all Gilda's attention was focused upon the figure that stood in front of them. It was that of a man, stripped to the waist, and he was standing with his face to the farther wall. His arms were stretched high above his head with his wrists tied to a staple sunk in the cave ceiling.

Gilda had found Martin!

5

Thrills in the Dark

Afterwards she realised how terrible was the mistake she then made. Having discovered that Martin was a prisoner in the cave her next course of action ought to have been obvious. She ought to have slipped out of the cave as quietly as she had entered it. It would have been easy then to untie the boat and row for Knapp Village. The chances were that she could have brought the police upon the scene before Meyer and his companion had realised there was anything wrong.

But Gilda stayed — to be near Martin. Meyer was speaking quietly, but the quietness only served to intensify the menace in his tone.

'Why go on being a fool, Kane?' he demanded. 'You are our prisoner, and the police and everyone else believe that you are dead. So nobody will be looking for you, and you stand no chance of being rescued. Your only chance of life now is to give us the information we want.'

Martin's voice was a hoarse croak.

'I'll see you in hell first,' he said.

His voice wrung Gilda's heart strings. He was weak — ill. What dreadful tortures had he already suffered? And — and they were going to start on him again . . .

'What about Gilda?' demanded Meyer. 'Are you going to let her break her heart? Do you want to go back to her so disfigured that she will scream at the sight of you? You'd better give in, Kane. By this time you must know that we mean business and that sooner or later you'll be forced to tell us all that we want to know.'

'Do your worst!' Martin said. 'You'll get nothing out of me.'

Meyer laughed, the most cold-blooded sound Gilda had ever listened to.

'We waste time,' he said. 'Set to work, Max. I expect to hear him howling for mercy long before dawn.'

The other half-turned, and Gilda crouched back against the rock wall. If he caught sight of her now, she might not have time to get out of the cave. But — but she had to know what they intended to do to Martin.

Max did not look in her direction. Stooping, he picked up a short-handled whip and Gilda's eyes dilated at sight of it. There were several thongs to the whip and every one was studded with jagged pieces of metal. Such a whip would tear a man's back to shreds.

It was all Gilda could do to hold herself in check. If she'd had a gun she would have shot Meyer and his confederate and then gloried in the deed. She felt impelled to rush forward from her hiding-place and place her hands on the whip which Meyer was holding menacingly over her lover. She wished she were a man so that she could use brute force against these torturers. Then, after she had freed Martin, she would have wanted to be a woman, helpless in his arms. Martin's voice brought her back to reality.

'Violence won't get you anywhere, Meyer,' he said. 'You're a fool to have double-crossed me. If you'd played the game, I'd have given you fifty-fifty. As it is, you can flog as much as you like, but I shan't tell you anything, and if you touch a hair of Gilda's head, I swear I'll strangle you with my own bare hands.'

Hugo laughed. 'You're pretty securely tied up, my friend. I don't think you're in any position to talk about strangling. Now why not be sensible — take the easy way out.'

'I'll see you in blazes first, Meyer! You'll have to commit murder before you find those jewels — and you'll hang, Meyer. You're just the kind of man who ends on the gallows.'

Meyer's hand which held the whip trembled. Like most thugs he was a coward at heart. Now his fear enraged him and he longed to smash the man who had taunted him.

'For the last time,' said Meyer. 'Will you tell us what we want to know?'

'No!' said Martin.

Max gave the whip a trial swing through the air. The mere sound of it set Gilda trembling. The man stepped close to his victim, then raised the whip high above his head. The thongs whistled through the air. There was the dreadful sound of impact and Martin's back was crisscrossed with lines of jagged red.

Gilda screamed. Hugo Meyer spun on his heels while Max let the whip fall to the ground.

They saw her then — standing clear against the moonlight outside the cave. Max, his nerve gone for the moment, crouched back against the rock wall. A jumble of words, in a foreign tongue, escaped him.

'*It's the girl!*' shouted Hugo Meyer. 'She must have followed us. Get her, man — *get her!*'

He came running forward but not before Gilda had already turned. She had done what she had set out to do because her scream had been born of cool purpose as much as of horror. Meyer and his companion now knew that Martin's prison had been discovered. They would be too busy now, wondering how they could escape the law to torture Martin further, provided always that she managed to get away in the boat.

Over the slippery stones she ran with her bare feet. She gained the boat and one quick jerk of the painter was enough to free it from a spar of rock. It swung away from the cliff face, and she pushed out the oars just as Meyer raced out of the cave. A furious exclamation burst from him, and Gilda saw the moonlight glitter on a drawn gun.

'Bring that boat back!' Meyer snarled.

The blades dug into the water and slowly the boat gathered way. Gilda was terrified that Meyer might either jump or swim for the boat. He did neither. She knew fresh hope; if Meyer could not swim, then she was safe. And Martin would be safe, too — unless Meyer used his gun.

Max appeared in front of the cave, and a gun also gleamed in his hand.

He levelled it, but Meyer struck it upwards.

'Put that gun away,' he snarled. 'This may be a lonely spot, but there's no telling how far sound will travel. We don't want people rowing out from Knapp to discover who's doing the shooting.'

'But you can't let her get away,' yelled Max in terror. 'We're marooned here — we can't swim. She'll bring the police back with her. And — and I warned you about her — I knew something like this would happen. It's — it's just because you can't keep your hands off a woman . . .'

Meyer abruptly cut him short, but Gilda failed to hear the actual words. After that there was silence except for the creaking of the rowlocks and the lap of the water against the bows.

Gilda felt a deep relief. Hugo Meyer and Max were marooned in the cave; they could not swim, so there could not be any escape for them. They would do no further injury to Martin. Yes, she had been right to scream — to let them know of her presence.

Soon she would be comforting Martin. Her arms would be around him, and his lips would be against hers. Only a short while ago she had thought that she would never kiss Martin again.

Everything was going to be so easy now. Her quickest contact was Elias

Cobb. She would rouse him, tell him what had happened, and get him to go for the police. He would be able to carry the news much more quickly than she could. She would retrieve her clothes and then it would be only a question of waiting for the police.

The boat grounded on the shingle opposite the fisherman's cottage. She hauled it as far as she could out of the water and then she stumbled over the smooth pebbles.

A light was burning behind the curtains of the cottage window. Elias Cobb must have got up again. Had she been missed? Or maybe Elias intended to do some night fishing.

Shuffling footsteps answered her knock at the door. In her excitement she forgot the door was not bolted. It opened and Elias Cobb stood there.

At sight of her, his jaw dropped and his eyes grew wide. For the moment Gilda had completely forgotten her state of undress.

'Saints alive, miss! I thought you were safe in bed.'

'Oh, Mr. Cobb,' she burst out. 'A most

wonderful thing has happened. I've found Martin; he isn't dead. He — he's being held a prisoner in the cave and that man, Meyer, is behind it all. But let me come in and I'll tell you everything.'

He still stood there and Gilda had to push near him in order to enter the kitchen. He followed and stood with his back against the door.

'What are you trying to tell me?' he demanded in his harsh voice.

In her excitement Gilda pitched her voice higher than usual. She told of the conversation she had overheard in the cottage, of her swim to the cave and what she had seen there.

'They can't swim, Mr. Cobb,' she went on. 'So they can't get away. But they've treated Martin so terribly that he may need a doctor. Will you please hurry to Tedworth and tell the police? You must tell them, too, that both Meyer and the other man are armed. Please hurry, Mr. Cobb — please!'

Cobb stood there, and he still made no movement. It seemed to Gilda that his dull mind had not taken it all in. Perhaps he did not believe her — perhaps he thought she had let her imagination run away with her.

'Everything I've told you is true,' she gasped. 'Please hurry.'

Cobb then moved but only because someone pushed the door against him. His sister, a dressing gown wrapped round her, swept into the room.

'What's happening down here?' she demanded. 'There's enough noise to waken the dead.'

Then she saw Gilda. Her eyes opened wide, and once again Gilda saw them fill with hostility.

'What are you doing here in that state?' she demanded sharply.

Gilda was forced to tell her story all over again because Elias Cobb still stood mute near the door. At the end of it, the other woman's expression changed. Concern took the place of hostility, and she crossed to Gilda's side.

'What a dreadful ordeal you've been through!' she said. 'And to think that Mr. Meyer should act in such a way! The other man must be the one who drives his car. Oh, you poor thing!'

She turned on her brother.

'Why are you still standing there?' she demanded. 'You know what to do, don't you. Hurry, man. Get a move on! The sooner you get the police, the better.'

His dull eyes seemed to light up.

'Of course I know what to do,' he rapped. 'I didn't quite take it all in at first. But I won't be wasting any more time now.'

He left the room. His sister pressed Gilda's shoulder in a comforting gesture.

'Everything is going to be all right for you now, my dear,' she said. 'Elias is getting old; that's why he is so slow. I'd better go and hurry him up again.'

She left the room and for a moment or two Gilda heard the subdued murmur of voices.

The front door opened and closed.

The other woman came back to the kitchen.

'He's gone at the double,' she announced in triumph. 'You won't have long to wait now.'

Gilda suddenly shivered; for the first

time she was fully conscious of her state of undress.

'My clothes!' she said. 'I left them down on the beach near Martin's cottage. If you'll come with me I'll go and get them.'

Anna shook her head. 'I don't think it would be wise for us to go out, my dear,' she said. 'There may be more than two of them; others may be hanging about the cove. It'll be much safer if we wait here until the police come. And, in any case, I can lend you a house coat.'

She returned with the long garment, and Gilda wrapped herself comfortably into its warmth. Once again she wondered about Elias Cobb's sister.

She must be a woman of taste and extravagant habits; this was certainly the most expensive house coat Gilda had ever worn.

'I'll make some tea,' said Elias's sister. 'It'll help to kill time while we're waiting.'

The kettle boiled and the tea was made. It made new life flow into Gilda's limbs. But — even so — the minutes dragged. She knew the minutes would continue to drag until Martin was free, and safe in her arms.

As Elias Cobb's sister, Anna, fussed around, making her warm and handing the cup of tea to her, Gilda felt that she must have misjudged the woman. She was being kindness itself.

'You've been through a terrible ordeal,' Anna was saying. 'But there — it's all over now, my dear. Martin will be back soon, and then I expect we shall be having a wedding, eh?' The girl laughed melodiously. 'I'd love to be bridesmaid.'

'Of course, I'd be only too glad — '

'Mind you, I've never felt like settling down myself,' the woman cut in chattily. 'Somehow I've never felt that I could trust the men I've met. Maybe I attract the wrong kind — the flashy sort. Take Hugo Meyer, for instance. Well, I felt I could have fallen for him with the prospect of a wedding ring sometime in the future. But I guess I've had a lucky escape. He's turned out to be a thoroughly nasty bit of work, and women will be safer when that Romeo is put behind bars. I wouldn't have been in your shoes for anything, my dear.'

'Well, I don't mind telling you I'm glad it's all over now,' Gilda smiled. 'I'm counting the minutes until Martin walks in.'

'I don't blame you,' said Anna. 'Martin's one of the slow and steady sort. Those kind of men are best for women in the long run, I guess.'

'I know they are,' agreed Gilda.

Suddenly Elias Cobb's sister jerked up her head.

'Here they come now,' she said.

Gilda heard the sound of footsteps on the path. It couldn't be the police already. It had seemed a long wait, but it hadn't been long enough for Elias Cobb to get to Tedworth. Her panic died away almost as soon as it was born. Of course, somebody would have a telephone in Knapp village.

Cobb had phoned to Tedworth and the police had come racing by car. They were probably calling at the cottage before going to the cave. If so, she would go with them. She was determined that it would be her hands that would free Martin from his bonds.

A key rattled in the front door. There

were heavy footsteps, and Elias Cobb walked into the kitchen. He grinned at sight of his sister, and then stood to one side.

'Here they are!' he announced.

Gilda came to her feet — a flush of excitement making her fair beauty more glorious than ever.

Then Hugo Meyer and Max walked into the room! Both were smiling, and Meyer was idly twirling a gun in his fingers.

Anna caught sight of Gilda's horror-stricken face, and burst into peals of laughter.

'You little fool,' she choked. 'Do you still want me to be bridesmaid? Why I wouldn't even be a mourner at your boyfriend's funeral!'

6

Scream as Much as You Like!

Even then Gilda did not quite take it in; she still waited for the police to appear behind the two men. But there were no policemen.

Realisation came to Gilda as a physical shock. She saw the triumphant, sneering smile on Meyer's lips; she saw Elias Cobb's twisted grin. What a blind, utter fool she had been! Martin's safety had been in her keeping and she had thrown it away. If only she had stopped to think she would have been suspicious of the Cobbs from the very beginning. When Martin had disappeared, Elias Cobb had gone into the cave and had declared it empty although Martin must have been there. But she had had no reason to be suspicious of Cobb then. It was when she met his raven-haired 'sister' that she ought to have realised things weren't quite what they seemed. The woman's exotic appearance and her expensive clothes were obviously in keeping now — she was one of the gang.

What a fool they must have thought her when she had come to them for aid! Elias Cobb's fake stupidity ought to have warned her. She ought to have realised the hidden meaning behind his words when he had told his supposed sister: 'Of course I know what to do'. Instead of going to the police he had taken the boat and gone direct to the cave. No wonder the woman had refused to allow her to go and collect her clothes! If she, Gilda, had gone out to the beach she would have seen Cobb pulling for the cave.

Hugo Meyer gave a chuckle.

'So, Anna,' he said, 'I see you have well-guarded my sea nymph.'

'Since when has she been *your* sea nymph?' the other woman flashed at him.

So the woman was Anna Berg — not Elias Cobb's sister! She was Meyer's girlfriend — the woman he intended to get rid of as soon as the mysterious job was finished.

Meyer's dark eyes mocked at Anna, and two spots of red showed in her cheeks.

'Just a figure of speech, my sweet one,' he said easily.

His gaze came back to Gilda and she drew the house coat closely around her.

'It appears you made a slight mistake, my dear Gilda,' he said. 'Elias Cobb is a very good friend of mine. Knowing that, I wasn't too upset when you took the boat away from the cave. I knew it was a million to one you would make for Cobb's cottage. But for that, my dear, you would not have got away so easily. Much though I might have regretted it afterwards, I should have put a bullet right between your eyes.'

Gilda tried to keep her knees from trembling. The future held nothing but danger for Martin and herself now. The man who taunted her was a man without a soul.

Suddenly her tongue came away from the roof of her mouth and she turned to the woman.

'You must help me,' she burst out. 'I heard him talking about you. He's tired of you — he's going to get rid of you as soon as he's through here. He . . . '

The back of Anna's hand hit her full across the mouth.

'You — you cheap little slut!' she flared. 'How dare you! Why, for two pins . . . '

Gilda backed to the wall terrified of the talon-like nails that reached out for her eyes. But Hugo Meyer stepped in front of her.

'That will do, Anna,' he snapped. 'Can't you see she's talking nonsense?'

'It's the truth,' interjected Gilda. 'It's just what I heard you say. You're sick to death of her.'

He turned to her in exasperation.

'My dear Gilda,' he said, that hateful caress again in his voice. 'I must warn you not to anger me. I don't want to hurt you — at least, not until I have to.' He took a length of thin twine from his pocket. 'It's your own fault that I must take precautions,' he went on. 'If you had been content to stay asleep in the cottage, there would have been none of this unpleasantness. As it is, I must tie your hands.'

'I understand now,' said Gilda, coldly

and deliberately. 'You wanted me to remain in the cottage so that you could make love to me.'

Anna Berg gasped and again those tell-tale spots of red appeared in her cheeks. Gilda was glad. If she could only sow dissension — if she could only make them quarrel among themselves, then she would have scored a victory.

But Hugo Meyer still smiled calmly at Gilda.

'You have a very vivid imagination, my dear,' he said. 'Moreover, I'm afraid you flatter both yourself and your charms. But we have wasted enough time here, and I must take you to the cave now. It will be necessary to tie your wrists. If I have to gag you as well, it will be entirely your own fault.'

As he reached out, she swept his hands aside. She darted past him and was so quick that she nearly reached the door. But Max closed with her and he held her in a painful grip.

'We daren't run any more risks with this vixen,' Max said. 'Better make a good job of it, Hugo.'

'A good job it shall be,' said Meyer grimly.

Not only did they tie her hands and her feet, but they fixed a cloth round her mouth as well. However, Gilda had one faint morsel of satisfaction.

She had seen the smouldering suspicion in the eyes of Anna Berg. That spelled trouble for Hugo Meyer!

She was carried out of the cottage and across the shingle to the boat.

Meyer and Max climbed in after her; Elias Cobb and Anna Berg stood to watch while the boat pulled away.

As the two men carried Gilda into the cave, she saw the first promise of dawn lighting the sky. The storm lantern was still burning on the ledge, but Martin was now seated with his back against the wall. She saw the agony that came into his eyes at the sight of her.

'Gilda,' he said brokenly. 'They told me they would have no trouble in catching you. I dreaded it!'

Hugo Meyer set her on her feet, stooped, and pulled away the cord from her ankles. Her wrists were untied, and her arms were immediately pulled behind her back; then her wrists were tied again. She was forced to sit down facing Martin while the cord around her wrists was attached to a staple in the wall.

Meyer pulled away the gag.

'Scream as much as you like!' he said. 'But it's only fair to tell you that no sound will be heard outside the cave.'

Only the loathing in her eyes answered him. He smiled at her and then he turned to Martin.

'It's almost daylight,' he said, 'and so I'm going to leave you. You see it's not wise for anyone to be seen near the cave during the day; it might cause suspicion. I shall go, but Max will stay here on guard. Not that he will interfere with you in any way. You and your lover will be left in privacy.'

His smile faded and his voice became harsh. 'I shall come back tonight — to get what I want. If you refuse tonight, Kane, then the consequences of what will happen to this girl will be entirely upon your own head. I make no further threat now, but I leave you to think it over. Adios!'

He turned and walked towards the entrance. For a few minutes he stood talking in undertones to his companion and then he disappeared. Max stolidly seated himself on a ledge near the entrance and seemed prepared to forget the existence of his prisoners. Evidently they were to have ample time to discuss the matter between themselves.

'They told me you had arrived in the cove,' Martin said to Gilda. 'I wouldn't believe them at first. If only you had stayed away. Why did you come?'

She explained what had happened since her first meeting with Meyer in the train. She blamed herself for not having seen through Elias Cobb and Anna Berg, and for not having warned the police as she had intended.

'No one could blame you,' he said, and his eyes shone as he looked at her. 'I'm proud of you, Gilda.'

'But what does it all mean?' she demanded. 'Who is Meyer? What does he want?'

He moved a little as though his back was hurting him.

'You know how fond I am of deep

diving,' he said. 'Well, only last week, I dived off the cliffs. The water was very clear that day, and, going down, I saw a wreck stuck on a ledge. It seemed to be a large motor boat, and it was lying on its side. There was a deck cabin, and, by banging on to the side, I was able to look through the smashed window. Wedged in a corner of the cabin table was what appeared to be a small pebble. Well, I grabbed it before shooting up for air. That pebble was the diamond I showed you.'

Excitement crept into his tired voice.

'I went down three times,' he went on, 'and I saw that there were other 'pebbles' swirling about on the cabin floor. I knew then there was treasure on board the wreck. That was why I wanted diving gear; I couldn't get into the cabin without it. Then, as soon as I received the gear, Meyer and his gang turned up. Well, I had no suspicion of Cobb. I went fishing with him. Then, without warning, he knocked me down with a club. I didn't lose consciousness right away so he hit me a second time. When I came to, I was tied up in here.'

'But the side of your boat was knocked in,' Gilda said.

'Cobb probably did that on the beach,' he said. 'It would be their proof of my death if anyone started asking questions. Well, anyway, I hadn't been here long before Meyer and Max turned up. Meyer was very frank. He told me the full story of the wreck.'

'To get your confidence, eh?'

Martin nodded. 'The story goes way back to 1940,' he went on. 'Governments of nearly every other country were fleeing from the Continent. The motor launch carried a government party, and with them they had part of the government treasure. Meyer declares it's in the neighbourhood of a million pounds — jewels and gold. Meyer and Max were the crew, apart from the skipper. The skipper knew this lonely part of the coast and that's why he came to Knapp Cove. But, crossing the Channel, the government men were murdered. On reaching the cove, the skipper deliberately sunk the boat, treasure and all. You see he wanted it broadcast that the boat had sunk with all hands when crossing the Channel. He intended to come back later and lift the treasure. But he reckoned without his crew. They wanted the treasure for themselves, so they murdered the skipper before he could set foot on shore.'

Gilda shuddered although it came as no shock to her that Hugo Meyer was a murderer.

'Meyer and the others would have been back for the treasure long ago,' Martin said, 'if they both hadn't been sent to prison for five years. Oh, yes, Meyer told me all about it. But there was one thing they overlooked. The skipper who sank the boat knew this part of the coast like the palm of his hand. He must have known all about the ledge on which the wreck is lying. But neither Meyer nor Max knew anything about the bay, and they were afraid to employ divers because that would have called attention to the bay. That also explains why they got Elias Cobb to work for them. It was his job to try to locate the wreck. I beat him to it, however. Somehow he got wise to what I was after — maybe he spied on me in the cottage — and he brought Meyer and the others down here post haste. Now they're trying to force me to tell them the exact location of the wreck.'

His broad shoulders drooped.

'I nearly got away tonight,' he added. 'I broke free and threw Cobb into the sea. But Max struck me down before I could dive.'

So it was Cobb who had screamed!

As Gilda listened to Martin, horror took possession of her.

'Martin,' she said quietly. 'No matter what they do to me tonight, you mustn't give in to them.'

His eyes searched hers.

'In mercy's name why not?'

'Because they'll never let us live to talk about the treasure,' she said grimly. 'The moment you tell them where to find the wreck, you sign our death warrants!'

'Good heavens, you're right, Gilda,' Martin agreed. 'God! How I wish I'd never got you mixed up in this. It's what comes of going after easy money — I figured, well — that we'd have enough to build a nice house and settle down. I wasn't after wealth. I just wanted to give you the best of everything.'

'It was only you I wanted,' Gilda said dully. 'Darling, all the money in the world wouldn't matter if only you and I could be together.'

She saw him, struggling at his bonds, and she pulled at hers, too, but they only became tighter.

'Oh, Gilda, it's agony, knowing that you're so near to me,' he groaned. 'That rat, Meyer, knows how we feel. This is his new idea of torture — a love torture — tantalising us by keeping us apart.'

She tried to say comforting words to Martin, but she knew she wasn't being convincing. Meyer was determined to break them — and when he learned the secret of the treasure, he would kill them, because dead lovers tell no tales!

7

Jewels of Love

During that day Max left them alone. Once, when Martin had fallen into a troubled sleep, Max threw a blanket over him and Gilda was grateful for that. Sitting huddled in the house coat, she tried to think. No matter what happened they were faced with death — of that she was positive. Yet there must be some chance of escape — there must! Was the problem too great for her woman's wits? If only she could think of a way! Several times she tried to hold her jailer in conversation but he ignored every overture. Evidently he had no woman complex such as Meyer had.

The shadows lengthened in the cave and there came the time when Max placed the lighted storm lantern on the ledge. Gilda shivered and felt that ice was forming in her veins. This was the beginning of the end.

Soon there was a grating sound outside the cave as a boat scraped against the rocks. Hugo Meyer came striding into the cave, his eyes glittering with excitement.

'We're starting work tonight,' he told Max. 'Cobb has brought up the other boat and all the diving gear.'

He turned to Martin.

'There'll be no more beating about the bush,' he said. 'Tonight, Kane, I mean business. So you had better think very carefully before you answer my questions. I'm not a Britisher. Therefore I am inclined to be, perhaps, a little more realistic about women. I know, too, that a man will suffer much whereas the suffering of a woman will break his spirit almost at once. Just think about that, Kane.'

He moved nearer to Gilda.

'In my country,' he went on, 'I have seen many a confession wrung from an obstinate man when the woman he loves has been in danger.'

Martin strained at his bonds.

'You damned swine!'

Meyer smiled calmly. 'First,' he said,

'for reasons that are entirely my own, we will try a simple method. Drag her to her feet, Max.'

Gilda struggled wildly and desperately. But Max was strong and held her easily. Hugo Meyer cut the cord around her wrists and then he tore the house coat from her shoulders.

'String her up, Max,' he ordered.

Her wrists were pulled in front of her and she was dragged to the farther wall. A cord was thrown through a staple above her head, and her arms were drawn up so that she was forced on tip-toe.

'The whip, Max,' snapped Meyer. 'Give her a dozen to start with.'

Gilda nearly fainted with terror. She bit her lip to stop herself from screaming. She visualised the deadly whip. In a moment or two those terrible thongs would be cutting into her back. She heard the horrible sound of the whip as Max tested it through the air. Then he stood behind her, and she knew that his arm was raised. She summoned all her fortitude to meet the blow.

'Don't do it!' shouted Martin. 'I'll tell

you what you want to know.'

A cry escaped Gilda.

'No, Martin,' she said. 'You *know* what it means. I'd — I'd sooner . . . '

'I'll tell you, Meyer,' he went on, unheeding, 'on one condition. That no harm shall come to Gilda — that she shall go free when all this is over.'

'They'll *never* keep a promise,' burst out Gilda. 'They won't dare to let either of us live. They'll . . . '

'Your conditions are accepted,' Meyer said. 'Once the treasure has been lifted, we shall leave for the Continent. That is why we have a motor launch outside the cave now. Cut her down, Max.'

Her hands were untied and she was dragged back to her original position. Listlessly she let them drape the house coat around her. There was nothing she could do now. By giving in to them, Martin had only put off the evil day. Of course their knowledge was too danger-ous for Meyer to let them live.

Martin was cut free of his bonds.

'You'll take us in the motor launch,' Meyer said. 'It's fitted with all your diving gear, diving lamp included. You understand diving so you'll go down to the wreck for us. The sooner you bring up the stuff, the sooner Gilda and you will be free.'

They took Martin out of the cave and she was left alone. The time dragged by. It seemed she had been alone in the cave for hours before she heard the grating noise of a boat outside. Hugo Meyer walked into the cave. His eyes were black pools of excitement and, in his arms, he carried a small box that dripped with water.

'That boyfriend of yours tried to pull a fast one on us,' he stated. 'We'd scarcely moved away from the cave when he tried to overturn us. He must have had that in mind when he agreed to my demands. If it hadn't been for Max, he might have succeeded, but Max dealt with him. He's learned a little sense and he's made his first dive. This is the result.'

He placed the box upon a convenient ledge. Then, finding a hammer and chisel, he started to prise open the lid. Gilda saw him reach inside. Then jewels dribbled through his fingers — jewels that flashed and glinted in the light of the storm lantern. He lifted up another handful; they cascaded in his fingers like a water-fall of flame.

'Look, my dear,' he said. 'Just look! There was a time when these graced the person of Europe's most lovely queen.'

Despite herself her fingers itched to fondle the wonderful gems.

Hugo Meyer smiled down at her again and now his eyes were darker than ever.

'You can have these as the price of your kisses my dear,' he said.

Gilda looked at the wonderful jewels, then looked full at Hugo Meyer. Suppose she agreed to pay his price — what then?

'They're wonderful!' she heard herself saying. 'If only I could touch them!'

'No reason why not,' he said.

He jerked away the cord that bound her wrists. She was still helpless, however, because of the cord around her ankles. Then he dribbled jewels into her hands.

The mere feel of them thrilled her despite herself.

'If only they were *mine*,' she breathed. 'The things I could do because of them! I could give up the office; I could wear wonderful clothes; I could *travel* — oh, I could do all the things I've ever wanted to do.'

'They can still be yours,' he said breathlessly. 'None of the others need ever know. But you — you know what my price would be Gilda — your adoration?'

'I think I understand,' she whispered.

He was almost on his knees before her.

'Gilda,' he said passionately, 'you're the most wonderful woman I've ever seen. Never have I wanted to love anyone as I want to love you. Not only for now, but for always. With me, Gilda, your every desire shall be satisfied: the whole world shall be your playground.'

His arms went round her, and he lifted her to her feet. The jewels fell to the floor of the cave.

'Gilda!' he murmured. 'I have waited so long for this moment. Oh, Gilda!' His mouth crushed against hers. Her body became supple in his arms and, as he forced her back, she kissed him as though she were kissing Martin. Then suddenly she seized his arms and forced herself away from him.

'Hugo,' she said. 'Please — not here. When I pay your price, I want to be looking my best. I . . . '

'But you are beautiful now,' he insisted. 'You always look your best. And, my dear, I need you so much . . . '

'No, Hugo,' she insisted. 'Couldn't — couldn't we go to the cottage? It — it need only be for a little while. The others are busy at the wreck. We can be back here before they finish. I — I could lie in the bottom of the boat — they wouldn't see me then. You — you could tell them you had to go to the cottage for something. And in the cottage, Hugo, I — I will pay what you ask.'

He was a man crazed with passion. This wonderful girl — her face framed in its halo of gold — was offering him her favours. Max and the others need not know he had taken her to the cottage. Why should he hesitate?

'We'll go to the cottage, Gilda,' he said.

He swung her off her feet and carried her to the cliff entrance. Carefully he put her in the bottom of the boat, and then threw a rug over her. He rowed some

85

considerable distance and then the boat touched against something. She heard Hugo calling out to Max.

'I've opened the box,' he said. 'It's the jewel box and it's packed right to the top. Has anything else come up?'

'One more box,' came Max's voice. 'Kane's not fit enough to stay down very long; we have to let him have long rests. He's just gone down again.'

'Splendid,' said Hugo Meyer. 'I'm going to the cottage for some more tools. I'll be straight back.'

The oars creaked in the rowlocks again.

The boat grounded, and he pulled it up on the shingle. Then he lifted her out.

'I'd better carry you, my dear,' he said 'though it isn't likely that anyone will see us in the darkness.'

He carried her easily up the narrow path and then set her down on her feet. Looking about her she saw that a large car was parked quite near — the saloon that had met Meyer at the station. He saw what she was looking at and he chuckled.

'We shan't need that after tonight,' he said. 'We'll leave it as a free gift for Kane.'

He carried her into the cottage and led her to the settee while he lit the lamp. Gilda held on to her courage. So far her plan had succeeded. But would she be able to carry it right through? She must because, if she failed, then it would be the end of everything for her.

He came and cut the cord around her ankles. Again his lips crushed against hers, and again she kissed him as she would have kissed Martin.

But again she forced him away.

'Please, Hugo,' she said. 'I'm in such a terrible state. Let me go into the bedroom; let me tidy myself. Just look at my hair! Please, Hugo. You see I want my kisses to be something you will always remember — something so very, very wonderful. Light the small lamp for me, Hugo.'

His dark eyes never left her.

'It shall be just as you wish, my darling,' he said, 'but don't keep me waiting too long.'

He lit the lamp and handed it to her.

She entered the bedroom but she hesitated to shut the door tight behind her. If the door was slightly ajar, he would be less likely to suspect her.

Two candles were standing on the dressing table. Quickly she lit both of them. Then she took off the lamp chimney, blew out the tiny flame and unscrewed the lamp holder. She poured oil on the bed, across the carpet, and over the top of the dressing-table. She was going to succeed after all.

One touch with the candle flame and the room would be blazing.

A sound at the door made her wheel, the lamp still in her hands. Hugo Meyer was there, watching her!

'You — you vixen!' he snapped. 'So *this* is why you wanted me to bring you here. You wanted to set the place on fire to light a beacon that would bring people running here from miles around.'

He launched himself at her. She flung the lamp at him and turned to grab one of the candles. The lamp missed him and his arms closed around her. She fought with all the desperation of a cornered, wild animal. She used her feet, her nails and her teeth. But, inexorably, he swept her back until they stumbled over a bed-settee.

Her strength was ebbing. She could not struggle much longer. His horrible, leering face was near to her, and his hot breath stifled her.

'So you thought you'd fool me,' he snarled. 'But you're helpless now, my dear.'

Even then she twisted away from him — and saw Anna Berg.

Gilda looked up at Hugo, and suddenly her brain was clear.

'What about Anna?' she gasped. 'She loves you.'

'To blazes with Anna!' he exclaimed. 'She's just a raddled old hag!'

'Hugo!' Anna yelled from the doorway. 'You swine!'

Anna stood there like an avenging demon. Her raven hair was disordered about her face and her eyes, sunk deep in her pale face, glittered with the cold ferocity of a snake's.

'I *knew* you wouldn't be able to keep away from her,' she accused. 'For a long time I've been walking the beach. I *saw* you bring her ashore. I *saw* you carry her here.' Anna laughed hysterically. 'I might have let you have your way with her.' she went on. 'I know you can't resist a doll-like face. But she had made me suspicious. She hinted you were tired of me. I couldn't stand for that, Hugo. You could have loved your other women, Hugo, so long as you didn't tire of *me*. But now I know that you have tired, and that, Hugo, has been your greatest mistake.'

Her hand darted down — to pull a keen-bladed knife from her stocking.

'You shall *not* kiss *her*, Hugo!' she screamed. 'I'm going to make sure of *that*.'

He jumped up quickly and swerved to one side.

But Hugo Meyer was not Anna Berg's objective. With the knife gleaming in her hand, Anna ran straight at Gilda.

8

A Wild Woman's Jealousy

Gilda, too, had started to her feet, and that action probably saved her life. Realising the other woman's intention, she was able to throw out a hand and seize her wrist.

The woman's charge carried Gilda backwards and again she fell across the bed-settee. The knife struck once, but Gilda moved her head in time. She tried to twist clear, and slipped from the edge of the bed. Anna Berg came down with her, but Gilda lost her hold on Anna's wrist. At that moment, Hugo decided to take a hand in the fray. Suddenly jumping forward he seized Anna Berg by the shoulders. Exerting all his strength he bore her backwards.

'You crazy fool!' he burst out.

'And whose fault is it?' she shrilled. 'Ever since I first met you I've let you wipe your feet on me. But *you* — you'll never sneer about me again. I'm going to make you *pay* for all that you've done to me.'

The knife flashed at him and quickly he jerked his head away. The keen point drew a trickle of blood from his throat. In backing away he lost his hold of her, and she flung herself at him again. He tripped over a rug and measured his length, and Anna Berg fell too, as she again lunged at him. He caught the descending knife and then they rolled over and over as he fought to take it, and Anna fought to keep it.

It was Gilda's chance. As she scrambled to her feet she seized one of the lighted candles and then tilted it over. The tiny flame caught the oil on the dressing-table. Instantly a line of flame ran across it and then down the front to the carpet. Gilda waited to see no more. She ran to the door while Hugo Meyer and Anna Berg still fought on the floor. Reaching the door she pulled the key from the lock. Slamming it shut, she replaced the key in the front and then turned the lock. Hugo

Meyer and Anna Berg were now imprisoned inside the burning bedroom.

Gilda saw the big saloon outside the cottage. Darting to the car she opened the door and climbed inside. Her fingers felt along the dashboard and the tinny jingle of keys came to her. The ignition key had been left in the lock. She turned it and a tiny red light flashed on. Twice she pulled on the self-starter and then the engine burst into life. Next moment, a racing figure leapt for the running board, and groping hands reached in for her.

'No, you don't!' shouted Hugo Meyer.

She realised he must have climbed through the bedroom window. Well, he wasn't going to stop her now. Sheer instinct made her act as she did.

She saw his eyes glaring at her, and she swept her aim through the window, her fingers outstretched, stabbing at those evil eyes. Hugo Meyer screamed with the pain and fell back from the running board.

Gilda jabbed her foot down on the clutch and tried to slip in the gears, but they were different to the kind to which she was accustomed. She had put the car in reverse and it leapt backwards to the spot where Hugo Meyer had fallen.

He crawled out of the way just in time to miss being run over by the whirling wheels. Before she could find the right gear he had wrenched open the car door and flung himself on her.

'You tried to murder me,' he shrieked. 'You witch! I'll get you for this.'

His hands tightened until they became claws. Then they closed round her neck, and his thumbs felt for her wind-pipe. She pummeled his back, but he seemed to be made of iron.

Now she was dealing with a raving madman. Still more enraged because he thought she had tried to run him down, he had the strength of ten men.

'You're too dangerous to live,' he panted, 'and too beautiful. I'll know the joy of your kisses even while you die.'

His mouth clamped down on hers, and though she bit frenziedly into his lip, this only served to tighten the pressure of his thumbs on her throat.

She gasped for air, but his mouth was suffocating her. She realised that, in a few seconds, she would lose consciousness, and then there would be no hope.

Her clenched fists ceased their pummeling of his unresisting shoulders. She went limp in his arms. But meanwhile, her right hand was groping towards the dash-board cubby-hole, searching for some kind of weapon.

With dying hope her fingers moved across the smooth empty baize which lined the recess. Then, in a far corner, her fingers touched something metallic. A spanner. Her hand grasped it. With her ebbing strength, she lifted the weapon, then brought it down on the back of Hugo's head.

The blow was only hard enough to stun him momentarily. But it was enough for Gilda. She pushed him with all her remaining strength until he fell dazedly out of the car, and then she pulled the door shut.

Darkness had now fallen, and she couldn't see Hugo, but she could hear him fumbling at the car door in an effort to get at her again. This time she must get away. He was in a killing mood.

The clutch went in and the car jerked forward. For one dreadful moment the engine threatened to stall and then the car moved forward. Although she had not yet switched on her headlights she swung round the cottage, in the darkness and then turned into the narrow lane that led to the Tedworth Road.

Suddenly her headlights were blazing and, as the car gathered speed, it rolled like a ship at sea over the rough surface. Gilda was on her way to the police.

Half a mile back Hugo Meyer still writhed with pain. Anna Berg came running towards him, blood on her face.

'You fool!' she shrieked. 'You've let her get away.'

He turned on her — every muscle in his face working with baffled greed and rage.

'I have to thank you for it,' he yelled. 'She's gone for the police. You know what that means? We've lost everything. I daren't even go back now for the jewels I left in the cave. You — you jealous hag — it's you who've ruined me! What did the girl matter, you fool? She would have drowned along with Kane tomorrow, and I should only have laughed. That was all she meant to me. And now — you've ruined me. Well, the wringing of your raddled neck will give me some satisfaction at least.'

His fingers fastened round her throat.

'I'll be glad to swing for you,' he shouted.

The flickering flames caught the glint of polished steel. A silver streak and a choking gurgle sounded in Hugo Meyer's throat. His knees collapsed underneath him and slowly he crumpled up, his fingers clawing at the woman as he did so.

For the moment she stood as though turned to stone. A wild shriek escaped her and wildly she flung herself on her knees.

'Hugo!' she pleaded. 'Hugo! You forced me to do it. But you mustn't die. I love you, Hugo. We can still get away, Hugo. I'll hide you from them.'

He looked up at her. But the insolent assurance of his eyes was replaced by the glaze of death. She sat rocking herself over him. Flames burst through the roof of the cottage.

'Hugo!' Anna wailed. 'I was mad! I loved you too much. It wasn't the girl; it was because you'd grown tired of me. I can't live without you now.'

She came to her feet, and for a while she stood motionless. The light of the leaping flames played upon her raven hair. Again the flickering flames caught the glint of steel but the polish was rather dulled now. Anna Berg drove the weapon deep into her own heart, and fell across the body of her lover.

There was a roar as the cottage roof collapsed and a pillar of vivid flame shot skywards. Its garish light played upon the two bodies that lay outside.

★　★　★

Down in the bay Max and Elias Cobb had continued with their work. Carefully they pumped down air to the diver working below. Presently they received the signal that he wanted to surface.

His helmet broke the water and they saw he was carrying two dull-looking bricks in his hands.

'He's found the gold,' wheezed Elias Cobb, his voice cracking with excitement.

They pulled Martin aboard, and seized the gold. Both men took a brick each and they gazed greedily. It was only when Martin began to slip sideways that they remembered his presence.

'Get that helmet off him,' rapped Max. 'Don't let him pass out on us; we need a lot more work out of him yet.'

They unscrewed the helmet. Martin gulped for air. Elias Cobb slapped his face in order to bring him round.

'Here,' said Max. 'Drink this.'

He held a flask to Martin's lips. He drank gratefully and the potent spirit brought a little colour back to his lips.

'Where did you find the gold?' demanded Max. 'Is there much of it?'

Martin found speech difficult.

'I had to break open a cupboard,' he said listlessly. 'It's stacked with the stuff.'

The eyes of the two other men gleamed like yellow lamps in the darkness.

'Will you be able to bring it all up before dawn?' demanded Max. 'The sooner you finish the job the sooner the

99

girl and you will be free to go.'

Martin stared at him.

'I'm almost all in,' he said. 'If I go down again tonight I'll be dead when you drag me up again. I'm so tired I can scarcely lift my arms.'

Max made a gesture of impatience.

'We'll give you a long rest,' he snapped. 'There'll be time for one more dive.'

A startled cry came from Elias Cobb.

'*Look!*' he cried. 'The cottage! It's on fire.'

Max wheeled round. Against the darkness the cottage stood out in bold relief, every window a square of yellow light.

Behind them Martin had staggered to his feet. In his hand was the gold brick which Max had put down when he had bent to unscrew the diving helmet. Lurching forward he struck Max with it at the base of his skull. The crook swayed forward and fell flat on his face.

A yelp of alarm escaped Elias Cobb and he tried to turn. But Max was in his way and he almost tripped. That gave Martin his chance, and again he struck.

This time the brick made violent contact with the man's forehead.

Elias Cobb's face went utterly blank. Then he, too, pitched forward and lay still.

'An eye for an eye,' quoted Martin. 'You struck me when I wasn't expecting a blow and now I've returned the compliment.'

He turned to stare at the blazing cottage and tried to step forward. As he did so, the blazing cottage danced before him in fantastic fashion. The exertion of striking those last two blows had brought Martin right to the end of his tether. He clasped his head between his hands and then he tilted forward, to fall across Elias Cobb.

★ ★ ★

The police sergeant at Tedworth was more than surprised when a wild-eyed, disheveled young female burst in on him. But he mastered his surprise in order to listen to her story. After that he made things happen with speed.

Gilda and the sergeant came back to Tedworth in a fast motor launch, together with half-a-dozen armed policemen. As she crouched in the stern, a constant refrain hammered in her brain. Would they be in time?

Round the headland swept the motor launch. Gilda strained her eyes.

'There's their boat,' she exclaimed, pointing to a dark shape on the waters.

One of the policemen used a strong pair of glasses.

'There doesn't seem to be anyone on board, miss,' he commented.

Her fear made her hold her breath. Had they arrived too late? Had Hugo Meyer raised the alarm — had they fled? And had they killed Martin before leaving?

The motor launch circled towards the other boat and now most of the police were holding their guns in readiness. They drew alongside and she saw the three inert bodies.

'They're all dead,' she gasped. 'Martin's dead!'

A policeman stepped aboard. He bent

over the figure clad in diving dress.

'No miss,' he called. 'He's not dead ... Neither are these others,' he said a moment later. 'Both have been well and truly coshed!'

They transferred the three bodies into the motor launch, and Gilda took Martin's head in her lap.

★ ★ ★

In the early morning Gilda sat at Martin's bedside. When he opened his eyes again, he smiled happily, refreshed by his long sleep.

'It was the burning cottage that gave me my chance,' he told her. 'I have to thank you for everything. You were a brick!'

Martin opened his arms to her.

'The government will look after the treasure now,' he said. 'But there will be a reward and that will pay for our home and the wonderful honeymoon I promised you.'

She sank into his embrace and his lips crushed against hers. Now, she had no need to pretend, as she had done with Hugo Meyer. With that kiss she gave herself — body and soul — to the man she loved.

VICTIMS OF
BLACKMAIL

1

'You're late!'

Marcus Webb snapped out the words without lifting his head from his desk.

The rat-faced, stooping man who had entered the room rubbed his hands and nervously shuffled his feet.

'No, Mr. Webb,' Amos Mann said in his thin, piping voice. 'According to my watch I'm dead on time. I wouldn't dare to keep you waiting, Mr. Webb.'

'Don't argue with me. If I say you're late then you *are* late.'

'Yes, Mr. Webb.'

Marcus Webb leaned back in his chair and scowled at his jackal. Despite the scowl it was a strikingly handsome face. The eyes were probably the palest blue that had ever been set in a human face, and his fair moustache was most impressive. There were women who declared it was Marcus Webb's eyes that made him so strikingly handsome. There were other women — and there were many of these — who declared they were the cold eyes of a snake — the eyes of a man who knew no pity and no mercy.

'She'll be here within the next five or ten minutes,' Marcus Webb stated. 'You'll let her in and then you'll take up your usual place. Keep your eyes wide open all the time she's with me. Women can be difficult at times. Some of them love trouble.'

'Yes, Mr. Webb.'

Amos Maun rubbed his hands again and cringed more than ever. Then he shuffled noiselessly out of the room.

Webb's mouth curled in disdain for a moment and then he came to his feet. Going to the front of the desk he bent down and touched a secret spring. A cunningly-concealed door flew open, and reaching inside, he took out a bundle of letters tied with blue ribbon. His lips curled again, this time with infinite satisfaction.

'It's high time I realised on you, my beauties,' he said.

Going back to his chair he opened the

desk drawer and slid the bundle inside. Five minutes later there was a discreet knock and Amos Mann appeared.

'Mrs. Redmond,' he announced.

A woman entered the room, and there was something curiously hesitant about her steps. She was beautiful — with a fair loveliness that caught at the breath. But, underneath her make-up, was the pallor of illness and, under her eyes, the shadows of many sleepless nights showed darkly.

Marcus Webb's smile was the ultimate in charm. Leaping to his feet he pulled a chair forward.

'It's wonderful to see you again, Carla,' he said. 'You look more glamorous than ever. Do sit down.'

Her luminous eyes stared at him — eyes filled with intense loathing.

'I prefer to stand,' she said coldly. 'This isn't a social visit.'

He went back to his chair, and, the tips of his fingers pressed together, he stared up at her. The insolent, appraising gaze swept unaccustomed colour into her face.

'You are more beautiful than ever,

Carla,' he said in his soft, caressing voice. 'Even lovelier than when I first knew you. No wonder Hugh Redmond is so jealous of you.'

'We won't discuss my husband,' she said, 'if you don't mind.'

He shrugged again.

'But we must discuss him,' he declared. 'It's because of him that you're here. However, if you've carried out my instructions, he need not enter into the conversation again.'

Her fingers showed white as she gripped the top of her handbag. 'Suppose I had failed?' she asked. 'You'd never have carried out your threat, would you? Even a man such as you could not stoop so low.'

He laughed outright.

'There is no question of stooping,' he said. 'I'm a ruthless man and I need money desperately. Because of my need I came to you. Hugh Redmond is very wealthy and he's very much in love with his charming wife. Five thousand pounds is nothing to him. You, as his wife, could easily get such a small sum. I came to you, too, because of what we once meant to each other. If you refuse to help me I shall know it's only because your old-time regard has turned to vindictive hate and, therefore, I should have no scruples in carrying out my — er — threats.'

He realised the effort she was making to keep her emotions under control.

'Suppose I've failed?' she said quietly.

He came to his feet.

'In that case,' he exclaimed, 'a bundle of your letters to me will be placed in your husband's hands tonight. I don't need to tell you what those letters contain. But, if he should ever open them, Hugh Redmond will learn how his wife spent a holiday at a certain bungalow — a holiday that was followed by a much longer one in Paris. Having read them he'll know that his wife was nothing but a . . .'

'That's enough.' Her interruption was a cry of anguish. 'I — I've brought the money.'

She opened her handbag and fumbled inside it. Greed came into his cold eyes, but the next moment, his expression changed. He was gaping down the barrel of a tiny revolver, which Carla Redmond pointed at him menacingly.

'I didn't bring any money,' the woman told him. 'If I had done, you would only have cheated me. You would have kept back one or two of the letters so that you could hold them over my head and blackmail me again later on. But I'm in love with my husband and I'm prepared to risk anything for my happiness.'

He trembled when he saw how white her trigger finger had become.

'You're going to give me the letters, Marcus Webb,' she said. 'All of them. If you refuse, then I am going to kill you. I know where you keep your letters so you can get mine for me now.'

She half turned and a hand came over her shoulder to seize her gun wrist. It was wrenched so painfully that her fingers relaxed their hold on the tiny weapon.

It was Amos Mann who had disarmed her. He had come noiselessly over the carpet from behind a heavy curtain which hung against the farther wall — a curtain which concealed a secret door.

There was the paleness of death in Carla Redmond's face and it was obvious that she was on the point of total collapse. Marcus Webb had no mercy for her.

'So you didn't bring the money!' he barked. 'You little fool! Haven't you learned yet that I never make a threat I'm not prepared to keep? You can go back to your husband if you like but, if you do, you'll only be wasting your time. I'll send him your letters tonight and then you'll be out in the street — neck and crop.'

'But, Marcus, I — I couldn't live if Hugh saw those letters. I was desperate because I couldn't raise five thousand pounds. All I could manage was five hundred. But I'll find the rest if you'll only give me time.'

'Hand over the five hundred,' he snapped.

He snatched the bundle of notes from her.

'Now get *out!*' he snarled. 'Sniveling women make me sick.'

Outside, a demented woman was stumbling through the darkness. From her lips came a constant, almost incoherent murmuring.

'I daren't go home — I daren't go back to Hugh. What am I going to do? What'll happen to me? I'm ruined!'

2

Diana Russell sat in the far corner of Tony's Bar and she was deep in conversation with Marcus Webb. At this early hour of the evening the place was only half full so they had plenty of privacy. But there wasn't a man present who did not envy Marcus Webb because Diana was beautiful and she was new to Tony's Bar. Her dark hair was swept back from her wide forehead making a perfect frame to her oval face. Imps of laughter lurked in her grey eyes — wide-spaced eyes that seemed to look at life and find good in everything. Her nose was perfect and no man could look at her lovely mobile mouth without feeling a quickening of his pulses.

Yet, in Tony's Bar, there were those who pitied her.

'I just don't understand it,' said one man-about-town. 'You see a good-looker come into this bar for the first time and then, when you next look round, she's sitting holding hands with that rat Marcus Webb. It beats me how he does it.'

At that moment, unmindful of the attention she was attracting, Diana's eyes grew serious as she gazed at her companion.

'How long have we known one another, Marcus?' she asked quietly. 'It seems ages though it can't be more than a week, can it?'

'A week exactly, Diana.'

'The most glorious week of my life,' she breathed. 'It's been wonderful! I'll never be able to thank you enough.'

For the moment there was a faint stirring in the cold depths of his eyes.

'We've had a lot of fun,' he agreed. 'It's been grand going places together, dancing and dining out. I was so bored till I met you. It's because we fit in so perfectly, because we like the same things, that we've had so much fun.'

He looked up quickly.

'Why the sigh?' he asked.

'Did I sigh?' she queried. 'But there

— I may as well tell you. All along I've known this couldn't last. Another week or so and you won't want me.'

'Nonsense!'

'It's the truth,' Diana insisted. 'A few months ago I came into a little money. Instead of saving it I decided to have a good time while I could. I came to London and took a flat. But nothing exciting happened — not until I met you. Now the money is almost all gone which means I must give up my flat, move into cheap rooms, and find a job for myself. You won't want to be friendly with a penniless typist, will you?'

His hand closed over hers for a moment. The stirring in the depths of his cold eyes was now stark desire.

'My dear,' he said, 'You make it easy for me to tell you something — something I've wanted to tell you from the very first moment we met. But I didn't dare until now; I was too afraid I might lose your friendship.'

'You would never do that, Marcus,' she said.

'I can't offer you marriage, Diana,' he

declared, and his voice was soft and caress-ing as never before. 'I'm already married but it's a marriage in name only. I was tricked into marriage, and my wife refused to divorce me. I've avoided women ever since with the result that I've led a very lonely life. But you, Diana, could make me the happiest man in the world.'

He tightened the pressure of his hand, and her eyes became starry.

'I'm a wealthy man, Diana,' he went on. 'I can give you everything in the world you desire. All I want is to spend the rest of my life trying to make you happy. What difference can the marriage ceremony make? I love you and I think you love me. I've a lovely old house in Welgate Street, but it's too big for a bachelor and I was really thinking of selling it. But it would be the perfect setting for you, darling.'

'You — you wouldn't grow tired of me?' she breathed.

'How could I?' he demanded. 'As far as I'm concerned you are the sun, the moon and the stars. No other woman can ever mean anything to me now.'

'It's too wonderful,' she whispered. 'I

can't believe it's really happening.'

His speech became suddenly thick.

'Then you will come with me,' he said. 'We really shall start our honeymoon tonight?'

She bent her head so that he could not see her eyes.

'Yes, Marcus.' He just caught the words. 'I'll go anywhere with you.'

He would have burst into rapturous speech but she stopped him.

'I must get a few things together,' she said. 'I can't come to you just as I am. I'll have to see about giving up my flat, too.'

'Everything shall be just as you want it to be,' he said.

She looked up and smiled.

'I'll be going now,' she went on, 'but I'll come to your house at eight o'clock.'

'*Our* house,' he corrected her. 'I'll be waiting for you, Diana . . . Put on your nicest dress, and we'll go out and dine at the Savoy. It'll be our celebration dinner for the start of a wonderful new life. Come before eight o'clock, darling, if you possibly can. I shall be counting the seconds.'

119

A few moments later Diana stood outside Tony's Bar. She drew a shuddering breath of relief. The sound of that soft, caressing voice had made her sick! If she had been forced to listen to it much longer she would have lost her self-control.

Yet, strangely, she was pleased with the evening's developments. She was going to Marcus Webb's house to live with him as his wife. And she had very good reasons which prompted her to take such a drastic step.

Now she had a couple of hours in which to change and pack a few belongings. Then she must keep her promise to a man she hated.

Reaching the pavement she looked around her for a taxi. As she did so a car turned the corner and came slowly towards her. Suddenly it cut into the kerb and braked to a stop.

'Why, Diana!' greeted a very familiar voice. 'Of all people! I've been looking for you all over town.'

She blinked — could scarcely believe it was true.

Gerry Norton! She caught her breath at the sight of this childhood sweetheart who had squired her about her native village until she had suddenly left the peaceful spot to come to London on this dangerous mission.

'Why, Gerry!' she exclaimed, and, with him, she didn't have to fake the delight in her voice. 'It's grand to see you.'

He swung the car door open.

'Taxi, miss?' he joked. 'Hop in!'

'I'm in a hurry to get to my flat,' she told him. 'I've an important dinner engagement tonight and I don't want to be late.'

'It's lucky I recognised you,' he said. 'You might have waited ages for a taxi at this hour.'

They sped through several streets and then she lifted her head to look at him. She couldn't help comparing him with Marcus Webb.

Gerry was handsome in a rugged way — the way that a man should be handsome. The sun-tan of his face was something entirely different to the pink-and-white of Marcus Webb.

'Why did you leave the village in such

haste?' Gerry asked. 'Did you forget that we had a date on the Wednesday? I called for you and they told me you'd gone away. Nobody seemed to know where. It had me quite worried, Diana.'

She felt the colour sweep into her cheeks.

'I'm sorry about that, Gerry,' she answered. 'I didn't forget the date but I was called away in a hurry. It was a matter of business that couldn't be put off.'

She knew he was in love with her and she had known it for months. She liked him very, very much but she wasn't sure that she loved him. The car drew to a standstill outside the block of flats.

Gerry turned to her in an impulsive way.

'Diana,' he said urgently, 'forget your dinner date tonight. Come out with me instead!'

So the situation was going to be more difficult than she had imagined. 'I'd like to, Gerry,' she said, 'but I just can't.'

'What about tomorrow?'

'I'm going away tomorrow for a very long while.'

His grip on her arm tightened.

'Then you've got to listen to me now,' he said and his voice was suddenly harsh. 'It's something I'd decided to tell you the day after you left Dilton.'

She tried to pull her arm away.

'Not now, Gerry,' she begged. 'I'm in such a hurry.'

'You've *got* to listen, Diana. I'm in love with you . . . have been for years. You mean everything in the world to me, Diana. I — I've sometimes thought you cared a little for me, too. Do you care enough to marry me? Oh, Diana, if only you would, I'd be the happiest man alive. Say that you do care — just a little?'

Some power beyond her control caused her to look full at him. Despite the gloom, he saw something in her face that intoxicated his soul. She couldn't hide her true feelings for him.

'Diana!' he breathed in exultation, and he drew her into his arms.

His mouth sought hers and still that strange power held her in its control. Her lips parted to receive his kiss, and her eyes closed in ecstasy.

Then abruptly — with an effort — she pushed him away.

'I'm not in love with you, Gerry,' she said. 'Even if I were, I wouldn't marry you. I would go crazy if I had to bury myself on a farm. I'm sorry but that's all there is to say.'

He was dumb-founded. Before he could speak she wrenched open the car door, climbed out, and slammed it behind her.

'Goodbye!' she called, and ran round the back of the car.

Only when her flat door had closed behind her did she start to breathe again. Panting, she leaned against it and her hands went to her heart.

She was in love with Gerry! The realisation had burst upon her when his mouth had crushed against hers. But she couldn't take the wild happiness he offered.

Unseeingly she stared straight in front of her. She must kill Gerry's love, because she could never go to him again — never, never! That night she was going to Marcus Webb's house to live with him as his wife. She had another plan but she dare not count on it succeeding. If it failed then she knew she was prepared to keep her bargain with Marcus Webb. To that her mind was fully made up.

3

Despite her resolution it was some time before Diana could force herself to start the preparations for the evening. Finally she packed a few belongings in a small suitcase. Then she set about the task of changing her clothes.

Further time was wasted over the choosing of an evening gown. At last she decided on the flame-coloured one. It wasn't one she particularly liked; it made her dark beauty too exotic. But it would probably appeal to Marcus Webb and that was all that mattered. She knew he was as much in love with her as it was possible for such a man to be in love. The more she could enslave him the easier it would be for her to carry out her risky plan.

Finally she had to make sure her handbag held three important items — the two tablets, the small hammer and the sharp-edged chisel. In the act of leaving she murmured a small prayer. It was a prayer that should her plan succeed, she would be able to return to her own flat that night.

She must hurry now because it was already late and Marcus would be impatient. If he had to wait too long he might become suspicious.

She must find a taxi as quickly as possible. It seemed she was destined to be lucky. Only a few doors away a cab was standing. Evidently it had just set down a passenger.

'Taxi!' she called.

It came slowly towards her. Giving the number of the house in Welgate Street to the driver she lifted in her suitcase and then climbed in after it. Swinging the door shut she settled down in a corner seat. Immediately a frightened gasp escaped her. There was someone seated in the other corner!

Before she could cry out, or attempt to move, thin fingers closed over her arm in a grip that hurt.

'I don't mean you no harm, miss,' a piping voice came from the darkness. 'I want to save you from harm. That's why

I've been waiting for you.'

Maybe it was the weakness of the man's voice that restored Diana's courage. The man in the cab seemed to be smaller than herself though she could see little in the gloom except the gleam of narrow, close-set eyes.

'Why should you wait for me?' she demanded. 'What is there to warn me about?'

The fingers clutched at her arm more tightly.

'You've just got to listen to me, miss,' the voice went on. 'I know all about you and I know where you're going tonight. I know that Marcus Webb is waiting for you and that you're going to his house now.'

She felt the hot colour flood into her face. How could this man know of something Marcus and she had discussed only a few hours ago?

'You must be crazy,' she said. 'I don't know what you're talking about.'

'Mind you, I'm not blaming you,' the voice went on. 'You're not the first young woman to fall in love with Marcus Webb. I've seen them come — one after the

other. Some of them last a month or so
— some of them only a few weeks. But
the end is always the same: out they go!
You're in love with Webb and you won't
want to believe me. But you must! I've
got something really terrible to tell you.'

'I won't listen to you,' Diana said. 'Stop
this cab and let me get out.'

The fingers hurt her arm now and she
felt a sudden twinge of fear. The unknown
man might be small but he was undoubt-
edly strong.

'You've *got* to know about Webb,' the
thin voice insisted. 'All his life he's lived
fast with women and young girls. He's
not wealthy as he says he is — he lives by
blackmail.'

'Will you let me go?' Diana com-
manded.

'Some of the girls part from Webb and
they don't cause any trouble,' the little
man continued. 'They meet other men
and they get married but they don't
escape from Webb. As soon as they're
married he starts to blackmail them.
Quite a number of them have died by
their own hands and I can give you their

names if you don't believe me.'

Diana shuddered. She didn't want to hear any more — she only wanted to get out of the car.

'But some of the girls have caused a lot of trouble,' the voice went on. 'Webb becomes inhuman then — he doesn't care what he does to get rid of them. And these poor girls disappear, miss — mercy knows where.'

'I don't believe you,' Diana exclaimed. 'Such terrible things couldn't happen here in London.'

He was holding both her arms in an effort to persuade her.

'Don't go to him tonight,' he pleaded. 'If you don't, I'll make sure he never worries you again. I — I want you to live to thank me — not hate me.'

But she had to go to Marcus Webb! Even if he was the greatest fiend in human shape she still had to go to him. Nevertheless, this man had terrified her. If her nerve deserted her now she would stand no chance of putting her dangerous plan into operation.

She turned her head to gaze out of the

window: the street was an unfamiliar one. So the taxi-driver had ignored her instructions — he was not taking her to Welgate Street! Of course, he was acting in league with her companion.

'Don't go to him tonight, miss,' the piping voice implored. 'That's all I ask. Stay away from him tonight and you'll learn to bless the name of Amos Mann.'

The taxi came to a stop at some traffic lights. Exerting all her strength Diana flung the little man back into his corner. To open the door and to snatch up her case was the work of a moment, but she left in such a hurry that she tripped over the kerb and fell on her hands and knees.

She was terrified then that Amos Mann would follow and pounce on her. But the traffic lights changed and the taxi jerked forward.

As she came to her feet she saw it skid round a corner on two wheels. For a long time Diana stood against some railings and tried to control her trembling. Her knees were so weak that she felt they wouldn't carry her a step forward, and, in her weakness, she thought of Gerry

131

Norton. If only he could appear out of the blue as he had done earlier that evening!

She cast the thought away from her. After tonight Gerry would have no place in his life for her.

She tried to get her bearings then. The district was an entirely unfamiliar one. It was a deserted thoroughfare, too, for she saw no signs of any traffic. She waited, knowing that sooner or later a taxi would appear. That was all. At long last a crawler appeared and she frantically signaled it. She made sure there was no man in the other corner this time. Recovering herself a little Diana wondered about the little man who called himself Amos Mann. Whoever he was he was someone very much in Marcus Webb's confidence. That was unusual in itself for Webb was not the type of man to share a confidence with anyone. He had too many shameful secrets.

One thing was certain: the man in the cab had hated Marcus with a deadly venom. He had made that obvious right from the start. Every time he had spoken the name of Marcus Webb his voice had been choked with loathing.

There was another thing, too: the little man had only wanted her to promise not to go to Welgate Street that night — he would not have minded if she had decided to put off the visit to the morrow. Why must she keep away tonight? It wasn't likely that Marcus Webb would change his character within twenty-four hours.

'I suppose he took it that Marcus would be so angry at my failure to turn up that he would refuse to have anything more to do with me,' she decided.

She saw then that the taxi was moving through the West End. Within a few minutes' they would be at Welgate Street.

The taxi came to a stop and she looked out to see that several windows in the house were alight. The street was one of very large houses, but No. 18A was an exception. It had been wedged in between two large mansions. But, being situated as it was in London's most fashionable quarter, the yearly rent must have been a truly amazing one.

Marcus Webb must do very well by blackmail!

Diana glanced through the window at the fare on the taximeter and then looked inside her handbag for the money. As she did so, the sound of a slamming door came to her ears. Jerking up her head it seemed to her that she saw a dark shadow dart out of the gateway of No. 18A. She certainly saw a figure run across the road in front of the taxi's headlamps — a roughly-dressed figure with a cloth cap pulled low over the eyes and a scarf wound loosely around the throat. Underneath the cap, Diana caught a glimpse of a face and the sight caused an involuntary cry to escape her lips.

It was Gerry Norton! Of that she was sure! The man who had darted out of the gateway of Marcus Webb's house — the man who had run in front of the cab — was her old-time sweetheart, the man she still loved.

What had he to do with Marcus Webb? He couldn't even know that the man existed. But then, it was more than strange that Gerry should have suddenly appeared outside Tony's Bar that evening.

Could it be he had known she was inside — that he had been waiting for her?

Her whole mind was in a whirl. First the strange man in the cab and now — Gerry Norton!

Slowly she climbed the steps. Every instinct she possessed urged her to turn and run away. The moment she pressed the bell she would seal her fate. To enter the house might mean death to the real Diana Russell for, if her plan went wrong, she would be an entirely different woman when she eventually left it — if she were still alive!

Her hesitation was only momentary. Up went her arm and her finger pressed steadily against the bell. She heard it ring somewhere inside the house.

The echo of it died away and she waited for the sound of approaching footsteps. In another few seconds she would have to play a part which called for nerve.

She lifted her hand to ring again and her arm stopped halfway as though suddenly paralysed.

From inside the house had come the sudden, staccato report of a revolver shot!

4

Tensing herself, she lifted her hand and pressed the bell push again. For maybe a full minute her finger maintained the pressure before she heard the sound of footsteps.

The door swung open, a shaft of light blinded her, and then she found herself blinking at Marcus Webb.

'Diana,' he greeted. 'I'd almost given up on you. I seem to have been waiting for hours.'

He was his usual immaculate self — more so than ever in his perfectly-fitting dinner jacket. The thought came to her that she had been imagining things — the running figure could not have been Gerry and she could not have heard the sound of a gunshot. The man in the taxi had upset her and, because of him, she had let her fears run riot. She forced calmness into her voice.

'I was involved in a taxi collision,' she

excused herself. 'Nothing very serious except that I've ruined my stockings. But it was ages before I could find another taxi.'

'Did you ring before?' he asked as he closed the door behind her. 'Both my servants are out tonight and I've been at the back of the house.'

She was tempted to ask him about the revolver shot but decided against it.

'I rang once before,' she said. 'But I haven't been waiting long.'

'I'm sorry,' he said. 'I've been half off my head with impatience and yet I kept you waiting.'

He piloted her into a luxuriously-furnished sitting-room — a room of subdued colours, wide settees and deep armchairs. He took the suitcase away from her, placed it on a side-table, and then held out his arms.

'Diana!' he said. 'At last!'

She suffered his embrace — allowed her mouth to surrender itself. She must not let him suspect her real feelings. After what seemed an age he held her at arm's length.

'I've changed my mind about tonight, my dearest,' he said. 'All this happiness came so quickly that I had no time to think. I forgot my servants would be away tonight — that the house would not be prepared for you. When you come here to live, my sweet, everything must be just right for you. So, for a few days at least, we'll stay at a hotel. It's what I should have thought of first of all because now we shall have a real honeymoon.'

She felt herself go icy cold. She couldn't carry out her plan if they went to a hotel. Everything depended on the fact that she must spend the evening in this house — alone with Marcus.

'I've a bag already packed,' he told her, 'So I've only to slip on my overcoat.'

They were leaving. Now — at once!

Her hand went to her head.

'I — I'd like to rest for a few minutes,' she faltered. 'That taxi accident shook me up more than I realised, and a drink would help.'

Instantly he was all concern.

'What a selfish brute I am,' he exclaimed. 'I'm so delighted at having you here that I can think of nothing else. Of course there's no hurry. And we must have a drink — we can toast the beginning of a new life.'

He went to a cocktail cabinet and splashed whisky into two glasses. When his back was towards her she slipped open the catch of her handbag.

Soda-water splashed into the glasses and then he carried them towards her. She had dropped into a chair near the side-table. Placing the glasses down, he seated himself facing her.

'You're not feeling really ill, my sweet?' he queried anxiously, and the anxiety in his voice was so intense that she wondered how this monster could so plausibly pretend to be sincere.

'No,' she answered. 'I shall be all right in a few minutes.'

He smiled and lifted his glass.

'Here's to the new life,' he announced.

Diana caught her breath. This was the end of her plan. If he drank the whisky too soon she would have no other chance to carry out her scheme. If they went to the hotel she would be lost. It would be impossible to put her plans into effect.

At that moment she happened to gaze towards a corner of the room and her eyes became circles of terror.

'Look!' she exclaimed. 'Over there!'

His whisky splashed down on the table.

'What — what is it?' he gasped, and his voice was little more than a croak. She saw real fright in his eyes then and she knew that, for some reason, he was afraid to look behind him.

'A mouse!' she exclaimed. 'I saw it. In that corner!'

The terror faded from the pale eyes.

'Nonsense,' he snapped. 'There are no mice in the house.'

Diana was standing up, still pretending to be scared.

'They terrify me,' she gasped. 'There really is one there — underneath that chair. Please — please get rid of it.'

She pulled her gown tight around her legs.

'I won't find anything there,' he smiled. 'You'll see that you're just imagining things.'

He started across the room. As he

turned Diana released her gown and her hand dived into her handbag. Then, quickly, she dropped two tiny tablets into his glass. They fizzed for a few seconds and then they were gone.

Marcus Webb pulled the chair away from the corner.

'I told you so my dear,' he said. 'There's nothing here — nothing at all.'

'I — I could have sworn I saw a big mouse,' Diana said, with feminine help-lessness.

He came back to the table and she smiled up at him.

'I'm sorry to be so foolish,' she said. 'But I'll drink the toast now. Here's to our wonderful new life.'

She gulped down the contents of her glass.

'To our wonderful new life,' he echoed, and he, too, emptied his glass.

'Another?' he queried.

'No, thank you, Marcus. I feel better now.'

'Then I may as well get my coat,' he said. 'If we don't hurry we shall lose our table at the restaurant.'

She shook her head, and again she wondered at his anxiety to get out of the house.

'I can't leave like this,' she protested. 'My hair is all out of place, my dress is crumpled and I must change my stockings.'

'I'm being very ill-mannered,' he said. 'I suppose it's because I'm drunk with happiness. You'll find the bedroom through that door. But, darling, be as quick as you can.'

'Only a few seconds,' she said, and she had to stop herself from running out of the room.

When she was alone she changed her stockings, smoothed out her gown, and attended to her hair. All the while she was listening. Then, when she started to repair her make-up, she heard a crash in the sitting-room. Her heart pounded and then it almost ceased to beat. So her plan had succeeded after all! There would be no need for her to live in the same house as Marcus Webb now.

As though she was sleep-walking she crossed to the door and looked into the sitting-room. She expected to see Marcus lying on the floor. But he was still on his feet and he was leaning heavily on the table. On the floor lay two smashed whisky glasses. His face had twisted into the ugliest mask she had ever seen, and, for once the cold, pale blue eyes were blazing. There was a maniacal fury in them — a fury that overshadowed the underlying terror.

'You witch!' he snarled. 'You — you put something in my glass. But you'll pay for it. I — I'll live to see you — screaming — for — mercy!'

The words choked in his throat as he fell forward on the table. It tilted over under his weight and he rolled almost to her feet before he lay motionless — his arms outstretched.

So the old sailor in the East End pub had played fair with her. She had told him she was being blackmailed — that she wanted to recover some letters from a certain man. It was the old sailor who had given her the 'knock-out drops.'

'They'll knock him out inside a couple of minutes,' he had said, 'and he'll stay out for several hours. It's ever so easy.'

It was going to be easy now — too easy. In less than ten minutes she would be leaving the house and she would be on her way to Carla. The letters would be in her possession.

Carla would find happiness again and, the fates willing, the terror of the last few weeks would have no effect upon her unborn child.

Going back into the bedroom Diana picked up her suitcase. Returning to the sitting-room she paused to stare down at Marcus Webb. For the moment terror clutched at her heart. Suppose the tablets had been too powerful — suppose she had killed him.

She moved nearer to him and found he was breathing heavily as though he was in a drunken stupor.

Crossing the room she opened the door on the right. There was darkness beyond but a faint, pungent odour assailed her nostrils. It seemed an odour that she ought to have recognised, but, at that tense moment, she couldn't place it.

She switched on the light and found

herself looking into Marcus Webb's study. The desk was in the middle of the room.

Carla had told her that the secret compartment was in the back of the desk. She would try to see if she could find the hidden spring. Not that she would waste any time over it. If she failed after a minute or two to find the spring she would rip open the back with the hammer and chisel which she carried in her handbag.

She crossed the study and began to walk round the desk. Suddenly she stopped as though she had encountered an invisible wall, and her hands went to her throat in an effort to stifle her scream. Behind the desk, a man was lying on the floor — his lifeless eyes staring at the ceiling. There was blood on the carpet and in the man's temple was an ugly bullet wound. In that very first second of terror, she recognised the narrow face and the close-set eyes.

It was the man who had warned her in the taxi — the man who had called himself Amos Mann.

She clutched the edge of the desk for

support. And, doing so, she saw something else — something that intensified her terror. Lying on the desk was a revolver she recognised. It belonged to Gerry Norton — the man she loved.

5

She couldn't be mistaken about it. It was his old service weapon — the one she had handled so often when he had been teaching her to shoot.

Gerry's gun!

Then she *had* seen Gerry running away from the house, and she had heard the sound of a shot. Now she knew that the pungent odour in the room was the smell of spent powder.

But she had seen Gerry running away, long before she had heard the sound of the shot, and Marcus Webb had known about the dead body in the study. Amos Mann's body was the explanation of Marcus Webb's desire to hurry her away from the house. It explained, too, the look of terror she had seen in the depths of his eyes.

She forced herself to look down at the dead man. It was incredible to think that, within the last hour, he had been alive

— that he had been talking to her. After she had left the taxi he must have come straight here. Death must have come to him very quickly because he could not have reached Welgate Street many minutes before her.

Had Marcus Webb killed Amos? The body must have been still warm when Marcus let her into the house. Despite the fact that he had murder on his soul he had intended to take her to a hotel to dine and dance.

She felt herself begin to tremble. Every instinct she possessed urged her to flee from this house of murder. If the police ever learned of her presence on the scene she would be dragged into the court proceedings. Everything would come out then and the newspapers would fill their pages with sensation. Instead of helping Carla she would be responsible for ruining her life beyond all hope.

The thought of Carla steadied her. Nobody knew of the murder. If the shot had been heard there would have been enquiries long ago.

Well, there was one good thing; she had

nothing to fear from Marcus Webb. He would sleep for hours, being thoroughly drugged.

It was terrible to be alone in a room with a murdered man, but surely a dead man could not harm her?

She must do what she had come to do and then she would hurry away. The police need never know she had been inside the house.

When she left she would take Gerry's gun with her. If Gerry were implicated, then she would be saving him, too.

She was glad she could turn her back on the dead man as she stooped to examine the desk. The rear of it was perfectly smooth and there was nothing to disclose the existence of a secret compartment. Her fingers felt delicately over every inch but she found nothing that suggested a secret catch. If she was to succeed she must rip the back open.

She took the hammer and chisel out of her bag. With great difficulty she pushed the chisel between the edge of the back panel and the desk top. She levered but she could not make the wood tear away.

She drove the chisel in further down and tried again but still with no result.

At the end of ten minutes she had only a jagged panel edge to show for her pains.

Was she going to fail in her dangerous mission after all? Now she was terrified that Marcus Webb might suddenly come to his senses. If he did and if he found her at the desk there would be no hope for her. He would kill her and know no remorse whatever. Of that she was convinced.

She dare not fail. Unless she found the letters there would be no hope for Carla.

With feverish energy she began to attack the top of the panel. Time after time she drove the chisel home and then tried to use it as a lever. Still the solid wood remained firm. Along the top she continued to work. Then — suddenly — there was a slight 'click' and a small section of the back swung towards her.

By sheer chance she had operated the secret spring!

Her heart beating fast she bent down to peer inside. It was only a tiny compartment and it held four bundles of envelopes. She drew out the first one. It was tied with blue ribbon! She wanted to shout her relief aloud.

She had found the letters for she knew Carla's handwriting as well as she knew her own. Carla need fear no more. Without the letters Marcus Webb could do her no harm.

In the very moment of her triumph Diana felt her throat go dry and it seemed she was stifling. She realised she was no longer alone in the study with the murdered man!

Slowly she lifted her head, startled. She expected to see Marcus Webb. Instead she saw two overcoated strangers with soft hats pulled low over their eyes. Both of them were holding revolvers.

'Ah!' grunted one of them. 'Caught in the very act, eh?'

Diana felt that power of movement was beyond her, and yet her legs somehow carried her back towards the wall. She didn't quite reach it for she was suddenly brought up short by a large china urn.

'Steady, sister!' warned the other man. 'We don't want to get rough with you.'

Slowly — relentlessly — they came further into the room. An exclamation escaped one of them.

'What d'you make of this?' he said all in one breath. 'Just take a look.'

His companion stepped nearer the desk. For a second the man looked down at the body, his hard face registering no surprise.

'A fine kettle of fish!' he commented. 'An unconscious man in that room and a dead body in this!'

'And her ladyship standing over the body and trying to tear the back off the desk,' said the other dryly. 'A nice how-d'ye-do, if you like.'

'A very callous young woman,' commented his companion. 'But perhaps this isn't her first murder. Perhaps murder's a hobby of hers.'

Diana found her voice at last.

'I know nothing about him,' she explained, and the firmness of her tone surprised her. 'I came here looking for something that belongs to a friend of mine. I'll admit that I drugged Marcus Webb but that's all I did do. He had something belonging to me and that was the only way I could get it back. When I came in here this man was lying on the floor and he was already dead.'

The taller of the two men stepped forward to peer at the back of the desk.

'I see you found what you were looking for,' he commented dryly.

'No such luck!' Diana declared, and as she spoke she dropped the bundle of letters into the urn. 'The letters I wanted weren't there.'

The smaller man looked at the revolver on the desk.

'Here's the weapon, too, unless I miss my guess,' he stated. 'We've got an open-and-shut case here.'

The taller nodded and then he looked full at Diana.

'We're from Scotland Yard,' he said. 'We were given the squeak that something had happened here. I must ask you to accompany me and it is my duty to inform you that anything you say will be taken down and may be used as evidence against you.'

C.I.D. men! Diana had known it from

the moment the two had entered the room. Their appearance on the scene meant prison for her and a long, long fight to prove her innocence. Perhaps she would be unable to prove it. But, in any case, Carla's secret was safe for the moment. Even if she was kept in prison she would find someone whom she could trust and would tell them where the letters were hidden.

If only she had been given time to destroy them utterly!

'I've told you the truth,' she said, 'and I've nothing more to say now.'

The taller of the two seemed to hesitate.

'There's no point in keeping her here, Bill,' he said. 'You'd better take her down to the car and drive her straight to the station.'

The other looked at him for a moment. Then he grinned.

'O.K.', he said. 'I'll take her along.'

He jerked his gun at Diana.

'We'll be moving sister,' he said. 'And I'm warning you not to make any fuss because I don't want to put the handcuffs on you unless I have to. But it's up to you.'

'I've no intention of making a fuss,' Diana said quietly.

As she walked out of the room she wondered if Gerry would be dragged into the sorry business. His fingerprints were sure to be on the gun. But fingerprints were useless unless the police already had Gerry's and there would be no reason for them to take his fingerprints if they had no cause to suspect him.

In the sitting-room Marcus Webb was still lying outside the bedroom door and he was still breathing as though in a drunken stupor. She saw her suitcase on a chair.

'That case is mine,' she said. 'May I take it with me?'

One of the C.I.D. men looked at the case, turned and grinned at her.

'Why not?' he countered. 'If we're going to keep you inside you'll probably need it.'

Leaving the room she began to head for the front door but the man stopped her.

'We'll go out the back way,' he said.

'We'll attract less attention and, besides, the car is at the back.'

He directed her along a narrow passage. Going through the back door she found herself in a small yard.

The C.I.D. man opened a gate set in the wall and she stepped through to a dark alleyway. Directly opposite her was the dark shape of an official-looking car.

There was a sudden exclamation and a figure climbed out of the driving seat.

'Who've you got there, Bill?' it demanded.

'Shut up!' the other snapped crudely. 'We don't want to arouse the neighbourhood. This lady is just paying a little visit to headquarters. That's all.'

The gun jabbed Diana in the back.

'In you get!' snapped her custodian.

She took a step forward. As she did so there was the quick patter of running feet. Out of the darkness came a flying figure. The man with the gun turned with a snarl but it was a snarl that was never finished. A fist made crunching contact with his jaw and he went down as though he had been poleaxed.

A string of oaths escaped the other man.

'What's going on?' he demanded. 'Let me . . .'

The unknown man turned in a flash. Diana caught the flash of a travelling fist — again she heard it make contact — and the second man was down. The unknown man whirled towards her and strong fingers gripped her arm. And, suddenly, she was filled with an overwhelming sense of security.

'Run, Diana!' gasped a voice. 'I've the car nearby. Run for your life.'

It was the most wonderful voice in the world; the man who had come to her rescue was Gerry Norton!

6

'Tumble in!' he gasped. 'They'll be on our track in a moment.'

She ran round the car and the engine had burst into life before she settled into her seat.

'Keep a look out behind,' Gerry said. 'Tell me as soon as you see us being followed.'

The car shot away from the kerb and turned into another narrow street. Street after street followed in bewildering succession.

'Do you see anything yet?' Gerry demanded at last.

'No,' she answered. 'There's nothing behind us.

She heard his sigh of relief.

'Then we've made it,' he stated. 'I've never hit so hard in my life so maybe both of them are still out cold.'

He turned to look at her.

'Who were they?' he demanded.

'Well, they said they were from Scotland Yard.'

Gerry frowned.

'But you weren't going with them of your own free will, were you?' he questioned. 'I was almost sure one of them was menacing you with a revolver.'

'I was under arrest,' Diana told him quietly, 'for murder.'

The car swerved violently.

'Good heavens, Diana!' he exclaimed. 'You — you didn't kill Marcus Webb, did you?'

'I only drugged Webb,' she answered. 'But, when I entered his study, there was a dead man lying on the floor. He was an under-sized, thin-faced man. And — and then some men came in and pretended to arrest me.'

He whistled incredulously.

'Well, that beats the band.'

'And, Gerry,' she, wept on, 'I saw your revolver lying on top of the desk.'

He turned to look at her, and she saw the anxiety in his face. For the moment her heart contracted. Surely Gerry wasn't responsible for the little man's death? But he couldn't be. The shot had been fired after Gerry had left the house.

'This is no time for explanations,' he said. 'It's terrible that you should have fallen into the hands of these men. But they're not getting their hands on you again — not until we've had time to sort this matter out. You've got to go into hiding and, somehow, I've got to fix it.'

His frown became deeper.

'We'll go to my cottage,' he said. 'Those men had no chance to recognise me — no chance at all. Yes, you'll be safe in the cottage.'

He bent forward further over the steering wheel.

Diana was glad that he didn't want her to talk. She had been through so much that her nerves were in shreds. When answering his questions she had been terrified in case a fit of hysterics should take possession of her.

She just wanted to lie back and try and make her mind a blank. Through the suburbs sped the car, and Gerry was careful to keep away from all main roads. Diana had no idea of the direction in which they were headed. It didn't matter. Gerry was beside her and there was wonderful comfort in that knowledge. And, no matter what happened, the menace of Marcus Webb was over. She was still Diana Russell and not the pitiful wreck she would have become if she had stayed with Marcus Webb.

The last of the houses flew by, and now they were out in the open country. For mile after mile the hedges flew by and still the car sped on. She lost all count of time . . . Then at last they were bumping over the ruts of a narrow lane.

Presently the car stopped.

'We've arrived, Diana,' Gerry said. 'This is it — our dream home!'

Her legs felt weak as she stepped from the car. She saw the dark outline of a cottage but that was all. No lights glowed anywhere to denote the presence of other buildings.

'There's only this room and the kitchen downstairs,' he said, 'so it's easy to keep the place clean. We shall be quite cosy here.'

He closed the door behind her and drew the curtains over the small window.

'I'd like to know all about it, Diana,' he said, 'If I'm to help I must know everything. I may as well tell you that I think I know a lot of it already.'

Already she had made up her mind to be quite frank.

'Well, Gerry, you know, of course, that Carla and I are twin sisters,' she said. 'Few people realise it because we're so utterly unalike. Carla is fair — and I'm dark. We're unlike in most other things. Well, I've always tried to look after Carla. You see, I've always known that mine was much the stronger character. But I failed to look after her where Marcus Webb was concerned. He was too tough a proposition for me.'

Her fingers clenched.

'He met her when she was little more than a schoolgirl and flattered her outrageously. Carla lost her head completely and, to cut a long story short, for months she became madly infatuated. She lasted much longer than his — his usual women. But no woman could live long with Marcus Webb without discovering his true character. Not a woman like Carla anyway. She learned to loathe him, and she left him before he was ready to get rid of her. You know what happened after that. She met Hugh Redmond and she really fell in love with him. Hugh was crazy about her and they married. But knowing the jealous streak in Hugh's nature, Carla never dared to tell him about Webb. For the last two years she's been happy, and never so happy as when she knew she was going to bear Hugh's child. And then — Marcus Webb struck! Unless she paid him the sum of five thousand pounds he would send Hugh all the letters she had written him. Poor Carla became frantic. She tried to raise the money and failed. She went to Webb then and tried to frighten him with a gun. But one of his servants was in the room. Carla was disarmed, and Webb struck her before throwing her out. He gave her another fortnight to find the money.'

Diana's voice had become almost harsh.

'She came to me that night and told me she was going to kill herself. I got the whole story out of her and she told me where Webb kept his blackmailing letters.

She had seen him go to the secret drawer in his desk once during the time she had been living with him. Well, I decided to try and get the letters myself. I went to London immediately and, in Tony's Bar, I became acquainted with Webb. I called myself Diana Brandon and I pretended to fall for him. He reacted in the way I hoped and he asked me to live with him. I consented because it was the only way I could make sure of getting into his house.'

She told him all that had happened then.

'If I failed to drug him, Gerry,' she said, 'I intended to keep my promise to him. If it was the only way of getting the letters, it would have been worth it. You see, it was Carla's life or my good name. And, well, Carla is my twin and I, perhaps, feel a little more strongly about her than ordinary sisters would do.'

She turned to him urgently.

'That's why I had to be cruel to you, Gerry,' she said. 'When you kissed me I knew I was in love with you — that there never would be any other man for me.

165

But I had to try and kill your love because of what might have happened to me tonight. I — I couldn't let you go on loving me if I had had to keep my promise to Webb.'

The expression in his eyes thrilled her intensely.

'I think I realised about your loving me when you kissed me,' he said. 'In fact I was more hopeful of winning you than ever before. Oh darling, I do love you so terribly!'

He took her into his arms and it was to Diana as though the night's dreadful happenings had never happened. In Gerry's arms there was supreme security and happiness.

It was much later when he told his story.

'Carla came to me, too,' he said. 'She was terrified of what Webb might do if he found you out. She told me about the letters and the secret drawer. I came to London and I searched for Webb. Early this evening I saw him in Tony's Bar and you were with him. I waited outside, hoping for a chance to speak to you. After I'd spoken to you, it was I who became terrified at the price you might be prepared to pay for the letters. I decided to break into his house right away. I climbed the fire escape and got into his study. He was there and I was almost sure he was alone. I held him up with the gun and demanded the letters. From nowhere, it seemed, a little man sprang at me and I was forced to drop the gun. There was a struggle — I knocked the two of them down — and I fled out of the front door. That is when you saw me. But how the little man died I've no idea.

'I think he intended to kill Webb,' Diana said quietly. 'He told me it would be all right so long as I didn't go to Webb tonight.'

'Perhaps he tried to use my gun,' Gerry said, 'and Webb took it from him and killed him. We may never know. But I was lucky enough to see you get out of the taxi when I was on the other side of the road. I saw you go to the door and I didn't know what to do. I was too sore with myself for having bungled everything to be able to think clearly. After you had gone inside I hung about and I was lucky to see that car go up the alleyway. I saw two men enter the back of the house and I just went on hanging about. Finally you came out; I saw something was wrong, and well — I went into action.'

'Thank goodness you did,' Diana exclaimed. 'You certainly are my lucky star, Gerry.'

Lying in his arms she found it difficult to concentrate on the dangerous problems which faced them.

'But what are we going to do now, Gerry?' she asked.

His mouth became determined.

'Just nothing,' he told her. 'We'll remain in hiding here and see what the police make of the case. The chances are they'll be able to solve it. If they do we'll be able to come out into the open and we may not have to admit that we know anything about it at all.'

'And if the police don't get anywhere?' Diana queried.

'We'll face that when we have to,' Gerry said. 'Meantime I'm going to see if I can find you some supper and after that you are going to your own room to bed, young woman. I want to see the roses back in your cheeks tomorrow.'

Next morning Gerry drove three miles to the nearest village in order to buy the morning newspapers. There was no mention of the murder in any of them. He went down again in the evening for the latest papers — still no news.

It was a wonderful day for Diana. Just to be with Gerry now was sheer happiness. Except for a nagging anxiety about Carla she wouldn't have had a care in the world.

There was still no definite news in the papers on the next day. But, looking through them in the cottage, Gerry found a certain interesting paragraph in one paper.

It was headed:

UNKNOWN MAN TAKEN FROM RIVER.

'Yesterday the body of an unknown man was taken from one of the lower reaches of the Thames. The face had been battered beyond recognition and a bullet wound was found in the head. Foul play is obvious. The man was elderly, below normal size, with thin grey hair going bald. He was wearing a threadbare grey suit, brown shoes, with white collar and black tie. Any people who know of a missing person answering to this description are requested to get in touch with the nearest police station.'

Gerry handed the paper to Diana and indicated the paragraph. She read it through and then looked up, puzzled.

'You — you think it was Amos Mann?' she questioned.

His eyes were bright with excitement.

'I'm sure of it,' he answered. 'The description fits him — hair, size, clothes and everything else — especially the bullet wound in the head.'

Diana was still mystified.

'But the police must have taken charge of his body,' she pointed out. 'They would have carried it to a mortuary.'

Gerry was striding up and down.

'I've been blind!' he exclaimed. 'Those C.I.D. men were fakes after all. I should have known they were phoney! When those two men entered Webb's study they were carrying revolvers. That's unusual for Scotland Yard detectives. No, my dear, they weren't detectives at all. If you ask me I'd say they were men in Webb's employ. He must have 'phoned them to come and take the body away before he went to the door to let you in. That would explain how they were able to enter the house so easily.'

Diana was staring wide-eyed.

'Yes, that's right,' she said. 'When the tall one said I was to be taken to the station the other one looked quite surprised. I had my doubts about them right from the start.'

'No wonder they made no attempt to follow us!' Gerry pondered. 'They wouldn't want to attract attention by a chase. I can understand it all now. They must have gone back to the house, roused Webb and then carted the body away.'

He seized Diana by the arms.

'This alters everything,' he exclaimed. 'We've got to think and act fast.'

Diana caught her breath.

'The letters!' she burst out. 'Suppose Marcus found them in the urn! Tomorrow is the last day of the fortnight he gave

Carla to get the money.'

Gerry's face became grim with resolution.

'I'm going to London,' he said. 'I'll get into Webb's house and this time I'll make no mistake. It's a million to one the letters are still in the urn. Webb will be positive they were in your handbag when I rescued you from his men. If the letters are in the urn I'll destroy them straightaway and then I'll go to the police. So long as we keep Carla out of it, there's no risk. We're in the clear now the body's turned up miles away.'

'I'll come with you,' Diana said.

He was firm about that.

'You've run all the risks you're going to run,' he said. 'You mustn't return to London yet. I'm not going to take any chances by letting Webb, or one of his men, set eyes on you. No, darling, you must stay here. Don't worry. I promise you I won't get into any trouble. With luck I'll be back before midnight. And, sweetheart, don't stir out of the cottage until I come back. You'll know it's me because I'll knock three times.'

7

Although Gerry arrived in London in the early afternoon he did not go near Welgate Street until it was dusk. Walking slowly down the opposite pavement he saw that a light was burning in the hall and also in the sitting-room. Someone was obviously at home. Having made sure of this Gerry made his way to the back of the house. Here everything was black. No light at all was to be seen behind the window of Marcus Webb's study.

'Here goes,' Gerry thought, and he climbed the wall that bounded the small yard. By leaping up he was able to pull down the fire escape into position. He swung himself on to it and went up almost at a run.

A faint sigh of satisfaction escaped him when he came to a stop outside the study window. As before his task was going to be easy for the window was open a little at the top.

Gently he lifted up the lower half. Parting the curtains he saw the thin line of light underneath the sitting-room door. If Marcus Webb was indeed inside the other room he would need to be careful.

Gingerly he climbed over the sill and, as the curtains fell together behind him, he switched on his torch. There was faint amusement in his eyes as the light focused on the back of Webb's desk. There was no sign of any opening but the marks of Diana's chisel were plain to be seen. The value of the desk as an article of furniture had been greatly reduced by Diana's handiwork!

Gerry was quick to notice that the room possessed a new carpet. Evidently Marcus Webb had taken no risks with the one that carried the marks of Amos Mann's blood. As the light of his torch travelled over it, Gerry also saw a small footstool and beyond it the large urn. He wondered if it still held the letters of the unfortunate Carla.

He listened and the subdued sound of voices came from the other room. So Webb was not alone. There was more need than ever for caution now.

Slowly he moved forward. Despite his care he walked straight into the small footstool. It tripped him up so that he staggered forward and then fell heavily across the desk. His torch rapped loudly upon the top as he fell.

From the inner room came a sharp oath and the sudden scraping of feet. The door was swung open while Gerry was still lying across the desk.

As he levered himself up the light was switched on and he found himself blinking at Marcus Webb and three other men.

Webb's revolver was already covering him.

'Good evening, gentlemen,' Gerry said. 'I apologise for disturbing you.'

The face of Marcus Webb was like a death mask.

'*You!*' he snarled. 'So you've come back.'

'Obviously!' Gerry retorted.

The three other men moved into the room.

'It's him right enough,' growled one of them. 'It's the guy who coshed me the night we grabbed the girl.'

Marcus Webb came close to the desk.

'Put your hands up,' he said.

Slowly Gerry obeyed.

'Frisk him!' ordered Webb.

The tallest of the three men ran his hands over Gerry.

'He's not carrying anything,' he reported.

'Good!' Marcus Webb snapped. 'Now tie him to a chair.'

Gerry was given no chance. Three pairs of hands gripped him and he was forced into a chair. His arms and legs were tied so tightly that the cord cut deep into the flesh.

Marcus Webb stood in front of him.

'Try to shout or make any other noise,' he stated, 'and we'll stick a gag in your mouth. Now, if you want to live, you'll answer my questions.'

Gerry looked at him challengingly.

'So you want to commit a second murder,' he said. 'You must be very anxious to swing, Webb.'

The other lifted his gun butt and for one second Gerry thought the weapon was going to smash into his face. But

Webb managed to control his anger.

'I guessed you were the man who got away with the girl,' he snarled. 'You failed to find what you wanted so you let her have a try. What did she do with the letters she took out of my desk?'

'Find out!' Gerry said.

'Where is the girl now?'

'Find out again!'

Webb's lips curled back in a leer.

'That's what I'm going to do,' he rapped, 'like this.'

His fist smashed into Gerry's face. Blow after blow he delivered until the young man's face was almost unrecognisable. Twice he knocked both Gerry and the chair over. He stood panting at last.

'Now!' he raved. 'Where is the girl and what did she do with the papers?'

Gerry spoke painfully through his bruised lips.

'Ask your grandmother,' he said.

Marcus Webb raised his fist again. One of the other men stepped forward.

'You'll only knock him out, boss,' he objected. 'Let me get to work on him. I know a better way.'

'Make it snappy,' Marcus said. 'Now that we've a chance to find the girl I don't want to waste any time.'

'Don't worry,' was the reply. 'He'll talk.'

The speaker left the room. When he came back he was carrying a length of cord and a thin copper rod. Walking behind Gerry's chair he placed the rod against the back of his head and then tied the cord over it and around the prisoner's forehead.

Just for a moment Gerry closed his eyes. He knew what was going to happen. Torture!

'If he screams we can still gag him,' Marcus Webb said. 'He can nod his head when he's ready to speak. Start working on him.'

The man at the back of the chair slowly twisted the rod so that the cord began to bite into the flesh.

'Don't be in any hurry, smart guy,' he said. 'I'm enjoying myself.'

He turned the rod again. Flesh bulged over the cord and perspiration streamed down Gerry's face.

Marcus Webb bent close.

'Where's the girl?' he demanded.

Gerry's bruised lips remained obstinately closed.

'Give it another turn,' said Marcus Webb viciously.

The rod began to twist again. Then a low cry burst from the sufferer.

'I — I can't take it,' he gasped. 'I — I'll tell you.'

'Ease it up,' ordered Webb.

The torturer spun the rod back.

'Now,' said Marcus Webb, his eyes like those of a wild animal. 'Where's the girl?'

'She's hiding down at my cottage,' Gerry whispered.

'Where's that?'

'Three miles outside the village of Rildene.'

'Never heard of it,' said Marcus Webb. 'Well, what's she done with the letters?'

'I don't know,' Gerry whispered. 'I think she's got them with her.'

Marcus Webb looked at his three men, blankly.

'I guess we'll have to believe him,' he shrugged. 'We'll put him in the car and we'll make him direct us. If he tries to double-cross us we'll croak him, and another dead body will go into the river.'

His face again came close to Gerry.

'Has the girl been to the police?' he demanded. 'Has she told anyone what she saw in this room?'

Gerry's lips buttoned up.

Marcus made a sign and the man behind the chair tightened the cord again. A groan escaped Gerry.

'I'm the only one who knows,' he gasped. 'She was afraid the police might be on her track because of the murder. She hasn't been outside the cottage since Amos was killed.'

'Say, boss,' said one of the others. 'Ask him why he broke in again tonight.'

Dark suspicion flooded Webb's face.

'Right!' he snarled. 'Put on the pressure.'

The cord drew tight.

'I came in the hope of finding my gun,' Gerry panted. 'I didn't want a murder to be pinned on me because it was committed with my gun.

The explanation seemed to satisfy Webb.

'Get ready to start,' he said to his men. 'We're leaving for the cottage right now.'

The tallest of the men bent down and examined Gerry.

'I'd better get him a drink, boss,' he said. 'If I don't he'll pass out on us and we shan't get any directions out of him then.'

Marcus Webb nodded.

The tall man poured half-a-tumblerful of neat whisky down Gerry's throat. The strong liquor did a lot to revive him, though at the same time, it made him slightly light-headed.

Marcus Webb and the others donned their overcoats. Then they untied Gerry and pulled him to his feet.

'Try to start anything,' Webb growled, 'and we'll begin on you all over again.'

'There won't be any funny business,' said one of the men. 'He's almost too weak to stand.'

Gerry was indeed swaying drunkenly on his feet.

Nevertheless, Marcus Webb insisted on his hands being tied again.

Two of the men half-carried Gerry out

through the back door. In the yard they waited until there was the sound of a car engine in the alleyway. They went out to it and Webb climbed in alongside the driver while Gerry's two guards bundled him into the back.

'If he tries to shout,' Marcus Webb said, 'stun him with the gun butt.'

But it seemed that Gerry had accepted the inevitable. He directed the car out of London and then along the approach to Rildene. When they got to the village he told them how to find the cottage. As the car swung into the lane Marcus Webb turned to him doubtfully.

'Will she be on her guard?' he demanded. 'I'm not taking the risk, she might suspect something is wrong and run to a telephone before we get her. Did you arrange to give her any sign when you came back?'

It seemed that Gerry's spirit had been completely broken. Only for a moment did he hesitate.

'I told her I'd knock three times,' he answered.

'Good!'

Marcus Webb's face became that of a

demon. He rubbed his hands in satisfaction. He was telling himself that, within a few minutes, he would have Diana at his mercy. Knock three times and ask for Diana. That was a laugh!

8

The day had seemed endless to Diana.
Hour after hour she reproached herself
for having let Gerry go back to London
alone. With the coming of darkness her
worry increased.

Suppose Gerry had fallen into Marcus
Webb's hands? The man was a ruthless
killer — he would murder Gerry if he
thought his safety was at stake. If only she
had taken a chance and gone to the police!
In matters like blackmail the police were
always discreet — they would have pro-
tected Carla's name by calling her Mrs. X
if there had been a court case.

Why, in mercy's name hadn't she
insisted on Gerry going immediately to
the local police station?

She would wait until midnight. If he
had not returned by then she would go to
the police herself.

When darkness came the hours seemed
longer than ever. All the time she sat

listening for the sound of a car engine.

When she had almost given up hope she heard it. So all her fears had been groundless — Gerry was coming back to her!

At that moment — despite her love for her sister — she never gave the letters a thought.

Gerry was safe! That was all that mattered now.

She went into the kitchen and turned up the jets of the oil stove.

He would probably be needing a meal.

There was a knock at the door and, for a moment, her heart stood still while she listened. Two other knocks followed. Gerry's signal. She ran to the door and swung it open.

'Oh, Gerry!' she exclaimed. 'I've been so worried, I . . . '

Her hands flew to her heart as a revolver motioned her back into the room, and, behind the revolver, she saw the hateful figure of Marcus Webb, accompanied by other men.

'Good evening, Diana darling,' he said and his voice was softer and more caressing than ever before. 'How pleased you must be to see me!'

The room was whirling around her. What had they done to Gerry? Then she saw Gerry as they pushed him into the cottage. The sight of his face made her forget everything else.

'Oh, Gerry!' she cried. 'They've beaten you!'

She would have run to him, but Marcus Webb caught her cruelly by the shoulders and swung her back against the wall.

'You stay *there*,' he snarled at her. 'Make another move and we'll treat you to a dose of the same medicine that he's had.'

Still watching Diana and covering her with the gun he spoke out of the corner of his mouth.

'Tie him up in one of the chairs,' he ordered his men.

Gerry was forced into an old-fashioned arm-chair and once again his arms and legs were tied. Webb smiled calmly at Diana.

'We're going to have a little talk, my dear,' he said. 'I'm warning you not to be obstinate or to do anything foolish. If you do, it's your boyfriend who'll suffer.'

There was no doubt he found the situation a most enjoyable one.

'I didn't realise the gang you had lined up against me, my dear,' he went on. 'You were very clever — the only woman who ever made a fool out of me. But I'm to blame. I'm growing careless. Right from the beginning, despite your different colouring, I should have noticed your likeness to Carla Redmond. Oh, yes, I know you are twin sisters. As soon as I discovered which letters were missing I made enquiries. I soon placed the attractive Diana Brandon then.'

His lips curved in amusement.

'You were clever, my dear,' he said. 'I was taken off my guard. I didn't think Amos Mann would ever turn against me. Years ago he tried to rob me and I caught him in the act. He told me some sob story of having an invalid wife — one who would break her heart if he went to prison. So I let him off on the condition that he worked for me. Very useful I found him, too — you see, he was always

187

worried about his sick wife. Yet you won him from me.'

'That's not true,' Diana said. 'I knew nothing about him. He came to me and warned me about you. He told me not to go near you that night. The next time I saw him he — he was lying dead. He was a stranger to me.'

Marcus Webb raised his eyebrows.

'It doesn't matter,' he shrugged. 'You also set your handsome boyfriend onto me. He held me up with a gun. Luckily — or so I thought at the time — Amos Mann turned up when I wasn't expecting him and he disarmed your boyfriend. There was a fight and your boyfriend managed to get away. It was then that the surprising thing happened. Mann picked up the fallen gun and menaced me with it. But I was too quick for him and it was Mann who died — not I.'

He smiled complacently.

'I telephoned my friends here,' he went on, 'and then you arrived. You played your little trick on me and you nearly got away with it; then your boyfriend had to come to the rescue. I tell you, my dear, I was quite worried for a while after I recovered from the effects of your drug.'

The smile vanished from his lips and his true nature was revealed in his face.

'And now you will answer a question,' he said. 'What did you do with the letters you took?'

'I destroyed them,' Diana answered promptly.

'You're lying!'

'I've told you the truth.'

He turned to the man who had tortured Gerry.

'Take your gun out,' he directed. 'Use the butt and smash it into the boyfriend's face. If she doesn't come clean we'll ruin his good looks forever.'

Callously the other man took out a heavy gun.

'Say when,' he said nonchalantly.

'Now!' rapped Marcus Webb.

The gun butt swung back.

'No!' Diana screamed. 'I — I'll tell you! Anything you want to know.'

Webb stopped the blow with a gesture.

'Well?' he demanded.

'They — they're still in your study,' she

told him. 'I dropped them into the big urn.'

Seeing the disbelief in his face she explained exactly what had happened.

'That's the truth,' she ended. 'I swear it.'

Gerry broke in. 'That's why you found me in your study tonight,' he said. 'I went back for the letters.'

Marcus Webb realised it was the truth and he started to smile again.

'That is really good news,' he said. 'My revenge now is going to be absolutely complete. Yesterday — most conveniently — my wife died.' His gaze travelled over Diana from head to foot. 'So, my dear,' he began, 'we are going to have our honeymoon after all. But it will be slightly different to what I'd planned. To start with I'm leaving the country. It was regrettable that I had to kill Amos Mann because I've no illusions about the police. They have no clues at the moment but I shall be safe only when I'm out of the country. We shall leave together, my dear — tonight. The ship on which we are due to travel will sail on the morning tide. We will be married by the captain.'

He turned to Gerry.

'But I don't think I shall need to be away long,' he went on, and then he spoke to the man who had tortured Gerry. 'You are not leaving with us, Bill, so you will be able to carry out the first part of my plan. When you go back to London you will take the letters out of the urn and post them without delay to Mr. Hugh Redmond. You will find his address in my book. By this time tomorrow night he should know exactly the kind of wife he married.'

A low cry burst from Diana. It seemed to afford Webb infinite satisfaction.

'But there is something else you must do before you leave here, Bill,' Webb continued. 'After we have gone, you will put a bullet through the boyfriend's head. You have his gun and that is the one you will use. Then, alongside the body, you will leave a crudely-printed note so that the writing shall not be recognized — to say that the boyfriend committed suicide because of remorse following the killing of Amos Mann. The police examine the gun; they will discover it was the same one that killed Amos, and that will be that! There will be a casual enquiry and, after that, it will be safe for me to return to England.'

The ordeal was no longer real to Diana. Such a fiend as Marcus Webb could not really exist. This was nothing but a nightmare — a nightmare from which she must eventually awake.

Bill only shrugged his shoulders.

'Just as you say, boss,' he said callously.

Marcus Webb, more pink-and-white than ever, turned back to Diana.

'We're going to South America — you and I,' he said in his caressing voice. 'We're going on a slow ship so that the voyage will be long. But the time will pass quickly enough for me because I shall have a lovely wife to amuse me.'

Suddenly the cold eyes were glittering and his voice was harsh.

'You won't enjoy it,' he snarled, 'because you've a lesson to learn. It is a lesson I teach all women who try to double-cross me. You will try hard to amuse me — very hard. Only by succeeding will you survive the voyage.'

His words beat against her brain but they made no impression upon it. She only knew she was surrounded by horror — indescribable horror.

One thought beat constantly in her brain. They were going to kill Gerry — they were going to murder him because of her.

'Oh, Gerry!' she exclaimed, and she started to run to him.

Marcus Webb struck her full in the face and she went down without a further sound.

Gerry struggled at his bonds.

'You — you inhuman fiend!' he shouted.

Marcus Webb ignored him.

'We're wasting time,' he said. 'Pick up the girl and carry her to the car. I guess I can trust you to carry out my orders, Bill. Fix everything as I have said and I'll be back on the return boat from South America.'

'I'll fix everything,' was the reply. 'Fixing this guy up as a suicide and leaving a phoney confession is just down my street, boss.'

The other two picked up Diana and they carried her out of the cottage.

Marcus Webb followed.

Gerry, with perspiration streaming down his face, gazed after Diana, and indescribable horror was in his eyes. There was something else, too — a dreadful puzzled expression. It was as though he had been confidently counting on something to happen — something that had failed to materialise.

It seemed, too, there was still expectation in his eyes — he was straining every nerve to listen. He heard the sound of an engine start up — he heard the sound of a car in motion. Quickly it died away.

A terrible despair showed itself on his face.

'It's all my fault,' he moaned.

His murderer-to-be looked at him and sneered.

'You've got nothing to complain about,' he said. 'You asked for it and now it's coming to you.'

9

How long she was in the car Diana never afterwards knew. At the very beginning of the journey she was bound and gagged. But pain and suffering no longer had any meaning — it seemed that her soul had died, because, back in the cottage, she felt sure Gerry had been murdered.

What did it matter what happened to her now? Now that Gerry was dead life had become meaningless.

The car stopped at last and, as she was lifted out, the smell of the sea came to her. She was hurried into a doorway, and, when a faint light was switched on, she found she was in a narrow passage. Up some steps she was carried and through a door into a well-furnished hallway.

'Take her into my room,' she heard Webb order.

From somewhere near at hand a woman suddenly screamed. She went on screaming.

'Somebody shall suffer for this,' he raved. 'What are they thinking about?'

The screaming died away and a low moaning took its place. Diana's blood seemed to turn to ice as they carried her into a well-appointed room and flung her on to a settee.

Marcus Webb came to stare down at her.

'You can give up hope now,' he told her. 'Nothing can save you from me. The captain is being informed that I'm ready to go on board and, as soon as my messenger returns, we shall leave this house. And; the moment you are on board, your punishment will begin.'

She was left to lie gazing up at the ceiling. The instinct of self-preservation took hold of her then and she struggled with her bonds. But she could make no impression on them — only to make them cut into her flesh the more.

Presently, Marcus Webb was back.

'Pick her up!' he ordered.

The two men who had been with her in the car lifted her as though she had been a sack. Out of the room she was carried and down a damp, evil-smelling passage.

They walked along this for a short distance and then Diana was carried to the foot of a flight of stone steps. Someone ahead lifted a trap-door and then she realised she was in some kind of a warehouse. Through a narrow door they took her and the cool, clean air of the sea ruffled her hair.

Across a narrow jetty she saw the towering side of a ship. Over a gang plank she was taken and it seemed to her that she was saying farewell to life itself.

Marcus Webb had indeed spoken the truth when he had declared that nothing in the world could save her now.

She was taken into a luxurious stateroom, and flung unceremoniously inside.

The two men who had carried her looked down at her with poker faces and then went out, turning the key in the lock. She kneeled on the floor, so tightly-bound that she couldn't move. In a daze she realised she was bare-footed, and hazarded that they had taken away her shoes and stockings so that any attempt at escape would be hindered.

Some minutes later Webb came into the room.

197

'I've come to keep my promise,' he told her. 'The captain's going to marry us now.'

Stooping he pulled the gag from her mouth. Snapping open a pen knife he slashed at the cords which bound her arms and legs as she knelt before him.

He laughed openly.

'Did you hope to escape?' he jeered. 'In a few minutes we shall be moving and your only escape then will be over the side. But that is not going to happen — yet. First you're going to be my bride.'

He turned, and her frightened eyes watched him twist the key in the lock. A desperate resolve came to her then. If he attempted to kiss her she would struggle so much that he would be forced to kill her.

Death was better than being his slave.

He stood over her kneeling figure.

'I'm waiting for you to get up,' he said.

She remained on the floor. She mustn't move until she was sure that the circulation had come back to her cramped limbs.

'I'm still *waiting!*' he snarled.

Suddenly he stooped and dragged her to her feet. Next moment a yelp of pain escaped him — she had sunk her teeth deep into his hand.

She saw murder in his eyes at that moment.

'You vixen!' he barked. 'For that I'll . . . '

From somewhere outside a whistle shrilled. Marcus Webb went suddenly tense. Above their heads sounded the thud of running feet, followed almost immediately by the staccato crack of a gun.

Anger gave way to fear in Webb's eyes. He flung her away from him, leapt to the door, and unlocked it. Opening it he stepped into the corridor outside.

Next moment Diana's heart was beating violently for a deep ringing voice echoed down the corridor — Gerry's voice.

'Better come quietly, Webb,' Gerry said. 'The whole ship is in the hands of the police.'

Diana shouted and she found that she could use her legs. She ran towards the door. As she did so Marcus Webb swung to meet her.

Before she could guess at his intention his arm had gone round her and she was pulled off her feet. For a fleeting moment she saw his eyes blazing madly. In his free hand he was holding a gun.

He lifted her out into the corridor and held her before him. Halfway down a companion ladder she saw two men, also armed.

Wild laughter escaped Marcus Webb.

'Go on — shoot!' he jeered. 'Shoot — and kill the girl. If I go, then she goes, too.'

His gun spat flame and the men scrambled up the ladder out of sight. Diana fought but she might just as well have used her fists against a brick wall.

Slowly — step by step — Marcus Webb carried her up the companionway and on to the deck. Diana saw many shadowy figures grouped round.

'Why don't you shoot?' Webb challenged. 'Kill the girl as well as myself!'

His gun barked again.

Men fell back before him. Suddenly Marcus turned and walked backwards. Horror took possession of Diana — she guessed what was going to happen.

Marcus Webb intended to throw

himself into the sea — and he meant to take her with him. The coming of the police only meant a quicker death for her.

'You'll never take me alive,' Webb shrieked. 'I'll beat the hangman yet.'

Because Marcus Webb was shielding himself behind Diana, the shadowy figures on deck were unwilling to fire. In the gloom they could not be sure of their aim. Even if it had been bright sunshine, only an expert marksman would have risked a shot. Webb drew nearer to the rails.

Then, out of the darkness, a figure came running. By the dim light of a ship's lantern Diana saw his face and a scream escaped her.

'No, Gerry! Go back!'

Gerry went on running towards Webb's outstretched gun. The madman recognised him, too.

'So Bill didn't kill you after all,' he said. 'All the better for me. I'll get you now.'

He fired. Diana screamed again when she saw Gerry falter and half turn. Then a mighty jump carried him forward. He crashed into Diana and Webb and all three thumped to the deck. There was the thud of running feet as the police closed in. But Marcus Webb was up in a flash. He fired once and then he swarmed on to the rails. He gave a horrible yell before his body tilted forward to disappear into the murky darkness.

Diana scrambled to her feet but Gerry lay where he had fallen — motionless.

She went on her knees, smoothing his hair with feverish hands.

'Gerry! Gerry!' she implored. 'You mustn't die now. You mustn't!'

But his eyes remained closed and it seemed that he had stopped breathing.

A policeman knelt down alongside her, and put his right hand inside Gerry's shirt.

'The bullet caught him in the shoulder,' he said. 'Don't worry, miss — I don't think it's going to be too serious. He wasn't in very good shape when he came on board with us. It's sheer exhaustion more than anything else.'

Gerry's eyes fluttered open then and he looked up into Diana's face. His hand reached up to touch her.

'You're safe,' he murmured. 'Thank heavens for that!'

★ ★ ★

At the moment when Marcus Webb's body was found, Diana was seated alongside a hospital bed and smiling down at Gerry. His shoulder was bandaged and his face a mass of sticking plaster, but otherwise he appeared to be in fairly good shape.

'There's a lot I don't understand,' Diana told him. 'They wouldn't tell me anything last night — they insisted on my going to sleep. Now give me all the exciting bits.'

He looked a little sheepish.

'I blame myself for it all,' he said. 'I oughtn't to have acted as I did without taking you into my confidence. I should have returned to the cottage and told you what I intended to do.'

'And what was that, Gerry?'

'Well, I thought it all out on the way to London,' he went on. 'I realised I was asking for trouble by breaking into

Webb's house. If I was caught the position would have been worse than it had been before. So I decided to go straight to the police. I realised they would understand about Carla and make sure that nothing came out about her. The police were interested as soon as I started to speak about Amos Mann. They had discovered his identity and they knew he worked for Marcus Webb. Oh, and another thing I — they had also found that his wife had died a week previously.'

'I think that explains why he wanted to kill Webb,' Diana said. 'Amos worked for Marcus only because he didn't want his wife to worry about him. How he must have hated Webb! No wonder he tried to kill him as soon as his wife was dead. Poor Amos loved his wife and he wouldn't have anything to live for after she died.'

'That must be the explanation,' Gerry said. 'Well, I also discovered that the police had been interested in Webb for some time. They suspected him of having something to do with the disappearance of several women and of being concerned in various rackets. Well — they were anxious to get tangible proof against him. Having heard my story they asked me to help them.

'To cut a long story short I was asked to try to trick Webb into making a confession. When I went to his house I was followed by detectives. On entering his study I deliberately made a noise so that he should discover me. You see, I knew that one or more of the detectives would follow me up the fire-escape and listen to everything that was said. And — well, I let Webb ill-treat me, maybe a little more than the police wanted me to. But you see, I had discovered exactly what kind of a man he was, and I reckoned it was worth it. Well, still carrying out police instructions, I told him you were hiding in my cottage and directed him and his gang to it.'

He smiled up at her.

'I knew it would mean a shock for you, darling,' he said, 'and I wouldn't have risked it if I hadn't been sure that the police were travelling close behind us. As a matter of fact Webb's car was checked through every town and village. Inside the cottage Webb did everything we wanted him to do — he confessed to the murder of poor Amos Mann.'

Gerry's face clouded.

'It was then that things started to go wrong,' he went on. 'After Webb's confession the police ought to have raided the cottage. But nothing happened. I knew then that something had gone wrong — that they had lost the trail. I — I just can't tell you how I felt when I saw them carry you out.'

'I was in agony, too,' Diana whispered. 'I — I gave you up for dead.'

He patted her hand reassuringly.

'The car had no sooner gone,' he went on, 'than the police raced in. Bill had no chance against them and they weren't easy with him. You see, they had overheard everything, and the reason they let Webb take you away was this: they suspected he was using a ship to smuggle contraband. That's why they let Webb grab you. They wanted to follow because they weren't sure which ship he was using. Well, I wasn't very far behind you. As soon as you were taken into that house at the dock-side, the police realised that the only big ship there was the one they were looking for. Guards were mounted and you were seen being taken aboard. The police raided the vessel as soon as they could muster, and well, you know what happened then.'

Diana stroked his forehead soothingly. She bent down her head so that he could lift his lips to hers.

'We'll forget all about it now my dearest,' she said. 'As soon as you're out of hospital, we'll be married, and then I'm going to spend the rest of my life trying to make you happy.'

He turned her face up to his.

'That goes for me, too,' he said.

It was a contract that was signed with a lingering kiss.

We do hope that you have enjoyed reading this large print book.

Did you know that all of our titles are available for purchase?

We publish a wide range of high quality large print books including:
Romances, Mysteries, Classics
General Fiction
Non Fiction and Westerns

Special interest titles available in large print are:
The Little Oxford Dictionary
Music Book, Song Book
Hymn Book, Service Book

Also available from us courtesy of Oxford University Press:
Young Readers' Dictionary
(large print edition)
Young Readers' Thesaurus
(large print edition)

For further information or a free brochure, please contact us at:
Ulverscroft Large Print Books Ltd.,
The Green, Bradgate Road, Anstey,
Leicester, LE7 7FU, England.
Tel: (00 44) **0116 236 4325**
Fax: (00 44) **0116 234 0205**

THE SEVENTH VIRGIN

Gerald Verner and Chris Verner

When Constable Joe Bentley rescues what he thinks is a nude woman from the freezing waters of the River Thames, his catch turns out to be an exquisitely modelled tailor's dummy stuffed with thousands of pounds' worth of bank notes. Later that same morning, the dead body of a man is found further downriver. Superintendent Budd of Scotland Yard, under pressure to prevent millions of counterfeit notes from entering general circulation, must discover the connection between the incidents, and stop a cold-blooded murderer on a killing spree.

A NICE GIRL LIKE YOU

Richard Wormser

Lt. Andy Bastian is back for his second scintillating case. This time, he heads a gritting and gruesome search for the man who violated a teenage beauty and left her just intact enough to someday tell the tale. But when his best friend becomes the number one suspect in the case, Andy becomes one of the star legal attractions. Without an alibi, things look bad for Andy's friend — but can Andy offer to help him and keep his integrity intact?